DORMANCY

A NICKY HJORT

Lavish
Publishing LLC

First Edition

Dormancy

2019 Lavish Publishing, LLC

All Rights Reserved

Published in the United States by Lavish Publishing, LLC, Midland, TX

Cover Design by: Victor R. Sosa

Cover Images: CanStock Photo

Paperback Edition

ISBN: 978-1-944985-88-2

www.LavishPublishing.com

Contents

Acknowledgments

First of all, I just want to say that this novella was so fun to write. An entire year lapsed between its writing and editing, and that rediscovering this story has probably been my favorite journey as a writer thus far. So…as usual, I would like to thank three people/groups and this time, unlike I usually do, will keep this simple and sweet.

I would like to thank the people at TPMG who gave me another way out of my life's loop. My family thanks you too. So much.

Secondly, I want to thank Pentatonix, some of whom not only went to the same high school I did (so cool—bragging rights— Warriors from Martin High in Arlington, Texas! Woot woot!) but make me weep with the unique and inspiring beauty of their music.

Thirdly, I want to thank Ted Chiang for writing the novella *Story of Your Life*, which affected my perspective of time and reality the way that the events of this story affect Jagga. And although many people loved the movie, *Arrival,* the true value of his story is in Mr. Chiang's written version. I'd like to think that reading this story might help his family realize how much his stories affected people like me.

Without further ado, I give you *Dormancy*. May it keep you up at night making you wonder what you are currently "buying" that you already possess within you and why the "Grid" wouldn't want you awake to the truth of who and what you really are.

In light and love,
    A Nicky Hjort

For Jeremy, my brother, who is wide awake in a sleeping world
and has...never once...been fooled by all its lies

Now I lay me down to sleep,
I pray the Lord my soul to keep,
If I should die before I wake,
I pray the Lord my soul to take.
Amen.

Prologue

I USED to think the worst thing that could happen to a person was being denied dormancy or being exiled off the Grid, but I was such a fool. Turns out that old saying about perspective being everything...was right. Something unspeakable, something far worse than exile has already happened to me. Too many nights to count, actually. And to think, I signed up for it. So did all the others by the way. It's funny how the very thing you think is helping you can be what hurts you most—before you get a clue, before you decode the whole program *they* are running or can recover from an addiction you didn't even know you had.

So many lies hidden in plain sight make them hard to see. Not many people know that because we forget so easily. One lie is easy to notice. But thousands, millions...not so much.

Unable to resist the pull of wanting to help so many others who, unlike me, don't know where we are really going...I look at the lines of us and shiver—lines and lines of thousands of AIPs, Artificially Integrated Persons, lines and lines of white lies disguised as perfect patterns, perfect illusions in perfect sight.

The chicken skin on my arms reminds me to look straight ahead, to help myself first, to not avert my gaze, to walk confidently forward toward my dormancy or...

Or else.

Chapter One

"Dude, move over. I am first to drop tonight. Move. My turn. Move!" My occupational partner, Faheem, smacks me on the back of my head, which even though it has belonged to me for thirty-plus years now, somehow always feels too big for my body. While I try to decide whether or not to take his crap tonight like I usually do, my eyes scan the perimeter and look for other pairs fighting like us. I see none. Probably thirty occupational pairs of same-gendered adults ahead and thirty-five dyads behind march side by side, pleasantly hoping to reach their dormancy pods as quickly as possible. That's only our line. We are flanked on either side by at least three lines of pairs, all wearing their Vantage-approved hooded jumpsuits in dull shades of blue, green, and grey—specific to their AIP class—behaving in a dull, Vantage-approved way. Except us.

His slap stings but only a little. Refusing to give him the satisfaction of turning, I keep my feet firmly planted on the concrete pavement as I laugh and shake it off of my acne-

3

scarred face and flip my dusty-grey hood onto my head. "Not moving. And it is so my turn to go first tonight. Piss off. I may be dumb, but I'm not stupid."

"Is that a fact?" He snorts and smacks me even harder on my left shoulder blade with that right hand of his, which I know almost as well as my own. The palm, both as wide and firm as the base of one of my fifteen computer panels in Persons Planning department, will leave one hell of a mark. "Well, I'm not as dumb as I look either." He seems grumpier than normal for drop-in tonight.

"Are you sure?" I say, still teasing him as I peer out on what must be a few square miles of flat earth, nothing but nothing in the distance beyond the electric fences decorating this desolate land of metal-lined refuge. I am sure as Vantage that this property looks like a massive stop sign with a cluster of buildings, both big and small, in the center from an aerial view because I have seen it. But I am not so sure he thinks I am as funny as I do. "Stop it already," I say, thinking about the number eight and octagons and the brilliant design of our Grid stations. *Eight, my favorite number even though I truly love all numbers.* "Math is so perfect. So elegant. So simple and clear. Don't you think?" I ask him, trying to distract him from whatever makes him so darn irritable before dormancy. That handsome dog is usually so cool and calm.

"Move. Jagga. I. Mean. It." His tone sounds serious. He keeps chopping his words into short sentences for the effect. "Me. First. Not. Backing. Down." He seems so much taller than six-four right now, and I am almost afraid of him, my best friend in the whole Grid.

I swallow, feeling so much smaller than five-four should. "Not moving either. You snooze, you lose." I dig my heels down and lean back into the hard walkway to get ready for another hit...because I know it's coming. Dropping into dormancy first and finally standing my ground with him would be worth it, though. Especially if it's not really my turn. Besides, tomorrow after my sleep cycle, I won't feel his abuse, and all the bruises will be long gone. So I can take all of his blows tonight like I'm a tougher man than I really am. Being a shrimp affords few luxuries in this life of bigger, better, or at least ideal efficiency…so I take them when I can. If I bend quickly enough, he will miss me altogether. It's worth a shot.

"No, you snooze, you win, Gag Jaaaaa." His drawing out the Ja at the end of the word almost sounds like a "*ya*," and he snaps his fingers to make sure I noticed how he turned the letters of my name into a new name.

I get ready to squat. Unfortunately, I'm distracted checking out the validity of his anagram, so I'm not fast enough to get out of the way. The painful blow connects directly with the underside of my shoulder blade in the same place, only much harder.

"F…" I pinch my lips tightly to keep the rest of the word from slipping out. "*Gag Ja*" *equals Jagga. Yep. It works.* I would smile, but I'm still too frozen from the pain and dig my nails into the cold metal railing in my right hand to keep from passing out. *Ouch. Really, ouch.*

The heel of his thick and muscular hand must have been pointed upward because the zing of the hit travels from my back up my neck into the base of my skull and then down again in cycles of pain that seem to grow before they let up, the concrete buildings in the distance blurring in my vision under the pain. After four cycles, I think I might die from the intensity of it, but by the fifth…the discomfort lessens slightly, and I accept that I will live long enough to make him pay for this. Surprised that the end effect of his smack could land so far from the initial impact, I reach out for the railing on the left side of this converging pathway to steady myself on both sides simultaneously as the final three cycles play out. My vision finally refocuses on the endless white concrete segmented sparingly with strips of light sand, rows of metal rods, reinforced electric fences, and plaster columns between, which seem to cover up some type of sensor, but no vegetation. Where did all the trees go? I wonder. Did they just *leaf,* or were they never here? I giggle at my own joke despite the pain. While I know there must have been trees somewhere on this damaged planet to sustain life before Vantage perfected the Grid, I see no evidence of plant life whatsoever before me, starving or otherwise.

I shake my head to gather myself, and one loose clump of hair drops down right between my eyes in between a flurry of stars. Like a pendulum, my lock of hair ticks back and forth, and I am mesmerized by the oddity of the color of it—not brown, not red, orangish, like a rotten carrot. I guess most of me is like some vegetable. My pasty, light brown, potatoey skin, pinto bean eyes, string bean legs, carroty hair, cucumber—the tiny Persian kind, mind you—shaped love factory that really needs some action.

"Gag," he calls out, shortening my name.

Now I've lost my "j" and my "a." Like that is supposed to offend me somehow. It doesn't. I lost the ability to be offended years ago, both because of homely looks and what I do every day. Disgust is a luxury no one can afford these days, not even amongst us—the richest of the AIPs here. There's just not enough time. But that's not why I am so quiet. I'm still trying to get my tongue to work properly.

Looking down, I stare in the general direction of my cucumber private parts and realize most of Faheem is more like a slab of meat than a vegetable. In the old days, he would be the main dietary attraction at a Churrascaria House for a hundred bucks a pop, and I'd be a wilted microgreen-salad disappointment at the street market costing about nine dollars, ninety-nine cents.

Now all AIPs are on the mandatory Vantage diet—mostly supplements, shakes, green powder, alkaline water, wheatgrass shots, certain omegas, and these caffeine/butter infusions to help us function as quickly, efficiently, and as long as possible. Cancer and acidity free. Thank G for that insurance policy. I hate the green powder we take three times a day no matter how many bacteria, viruses, and premalignant cells that its alkalinity kills for me. Yuck, just yuck... The way the stuff clumps in between my tiny but perfectly straight teeth... I miss real veggies, burgers, donuts, ice cream, alcohol—all of it banned now. I wish I could say I remember the way ice cream melts in your mouth. But I don't, not really anyway. I do remember remembering ice cream though—running to that pink truck after school, the woman on the southwest corner of Oak Street in front of Trussell Ranch Elem every Thursday afternoons at 2:38 p.m.—sharp. I wonder why I haven't thought about her in years. It's like I forgot to remember her until just now. Weird. *What else did I forget, and why?*

Ms. Debbie was never late. Never.

Come to think of it, no one is ever late these days either. One of the Vantage slogans plays in my mind so solidly as if I had written it myself. *"If you're on time, you're already late. So be early, your success mandates."*

"Debbie," I whisper the ice cream lady's name like she will rescue me from the wet-willie-loving bullies on the playground or the quiz I just failed (as if I ever failed a quiz) or the rattling in my head from Faheem's smack or...whatever. My ears tinkle like Christmas morning has finally arrived, and I can almost hear Debbie's old bell telling me it's time. It's finally time for a special treat. That bell was shiny like a new penny and reliably...no, perfectly pitched like the Pentatonix version of

"Mary, Did You Know?" promising us that neither she nor her Thursday visits would ever let us schoolkids and our snapping fingers down. I smile, almost too big for my beet-shaped face, because that a cappella version was always my favorite rendition of that song. Like stop me in my tracks and not let me move because the song took over and consumed me, the lyrics, who knows how many years old, still so beautiful and profound the way the vocalists sang them that they didn't need an instrument in the background. The words, in and of themselves, were enough for a number one hit. The words made the singers the melody, and the singers made the melody of nothing more than hums and swishes and claps. *Did you know?* I have never kissed the face of God. What's God? *Did you know?* Dang. I loved that song. *Mary, did you know? Yes. Yes, I did know.* I'll kiss the face of God one day too. *What? What is God?*

"Strawberry pop, please." The words just come right out of my mouth while I stand here, an AIP—just one of what must be over a thousand—in line, trying with all my might not to fall down from the pain bouncing around in my head. Yet even though I need it to hold me steady on these rails, my right hand reaches for quarters—to pay Mary for saving me...I mean Debbie—that aren't there, aren't in any pockets. Shoot. I don't even have pockets. Now we don't have pockets, public school, ice cream ladies, or quarters anymore. Now we have converging lines to dormancy, fields of concrete and steel, online education portals, smartphones implanted in our wrists, Vantage meal plans, and Vantage bucks that we access from our fingertips.

And we are always early. Always.

By the time I regain my ability to walk, Faheem is three paces ahead of me on this narrow path, which must be two feet wide but over a hundred meters long. Did he jump over me? Walk around? I can't be sure. All I know is he didn't step out of line. Once in the Grid, you never step out of line just like you never show up late. *Remember, being on time is already late, so be early. We never want to disappoint Vantage. Vantage, not Mary, saved us.* I scan round looking for any real signs of life and see nothing that isn't man-made. Where did Mother Nature go? *Did she leave? Or did we forsake her?*

The pain lets up a bit, and I am thankful I didn't squeak out a full-blown f-bomb. I look up trying to find the sun in a sky as clear as a never-ending blue banner, but it's never there. Lucky us here in the Grid, we have eliminated all sources of environmental pollution. Shame we traded the sun along with all the plants for eternal LED, extremely energy efficient and noncancerous, if not totally artificial and gloomy. I smirk, hoping some sarcasm will take the edge off the pain further. "Thank you, G." Curse words are vulgar and cause "unnecessary stress in the workplace." I flash back to the video we have to watch every year at Vantage Annual Orientation and Reintegration—*Four Forms of Violence in the Workplace*—the acting terribly overdone but the message clear: no weapons, bullying, lying to admin, or negative behaviors like using swear words shall be tolerated in this place without an immediate intervention by leadership. So when Faheem and I curse, we use anagrams to do it. There are no good alternatives to the f-word. So *fuck*, as far as we are concerned, is a barren wasteland of an explicative because there are no other words in it that make it useful to us.

I let go of the railing and take a step from one perfectly white concrete section to the next in my orthotic shoes that were designed to perfectly support and energize my feet, which should never be exposed to such useless and anxiety-provoking words as *fuck*. "Kid. Add c." I grunt. *Dick.*

"Ick. Add d. That also describes my favorite little prick." Faheem grunts back, exactly the same as I just did, and I can't help but laugh at how he just simultaneously mocked me in two different ways, half sort of apologized for hitting me, yet didn't violate the principles of that stupid video. If he wasn't usually such a gent, other than at drop, I'd probably not notice that.

Ick-d. Dick. Yep. Works too.

"Cucumber," I say, hoping my comment will confuse him. Guess I can mock him and kind of apologize at the same time too. I need him here. I need us to not be enemies in a world where he is the only other AIP I actually trust.

He taps his cheek, and that computer-like mind of his kicks in. "Cucumber—way better. Thirty-six words there. Only four in the one that rhymes with sick," he whispers before giggling, and I know the whole "steal his spot thing for drop-in" is as good as forgotten. Much like Debbie's ice cream truck before he smacked me.

"And none in the one that rhymes with duck. Duck that." I have to say that if I could take anything from the past into our present, it would be white rose bouquets and swear words. Bad words are just so fun to say. How can that be negative ideology? Whatever. Vantage must be right. They are always right. *"Don't worry; sit tight. The might of Vantage is always right."*

He leans over and laughs so hard he snorts.

"We need a swear circle, my mate," I say and laugh too.

"Duck. That. Quack." He grins from cheek to cheek, and I am sure I have him back again.

I go silent and take a big, deep breath because if he were a girl, I'd tell him he's my soulmate. I wish I knew how the Lamarwe coders paired us up as dormancy buddies because there is no way they could have possibly known we would both become obsessed with playing online chess and speaking in anagrams. All they knew was that we were the first two to mystify the Vantage Assignment Program, so they gave us the job of perfecting it and running it. Faheem and I are officially the only genius-level Educators, subclass CPP—City Person Planners.

We keep playing our little game of wordplay as we get closer to the drop site. Honestly, I don't want him to know how badly my head still hurts and that I am actually a bit nauseated…which is weird because he hit my shoulder blade. Why does my head hurt? And why won't that song stop playing on a loop like I'm an iPhone and my iMusic app has only one song on this playlist called *Mary*? Is it some hidden message? Who is Mary? Who is her son? I wish I knew.

"Nife," I say and snap my fingers. The nausea lessens, and I swallow my spit.

"Fine," he replies.

"Siks. S-I-K-S." I put one hand over my mouth and the other over my stomach.

"Kiss what?"

"My grits," I say like that means anything to anyone.

He laughs. "Your grits? What are grits exactly, anyway?"

"Massy. With two Ss. M-A-S-S-Y." *My ass.* "Grits were a southern food kind of like oatmeal, I think. Back when people still ate corn—before they knew about the genocidal GMO strains the US government had let loose in their mainstay food crops. What country kills its own people? Dude. Thank G for the Grid. Thank G for Vantage." Another one of the old slogans plays in the back of my mind, finally getting Mary and the great *I Am* off the damn loop inside my brain. *"If you have something to offer us, we have something to offer you. Vantage, vantage, the only sustainable option that will ever do."* I start to hum the tunes that went with the slogans, so catchy and cute. *"Don't worry; sit tight. The might of Vantage is always right."*

Faheem clears his throat and spits the mucous right in the middle of the thin strip of dry sand that separates our line from the next one over, now about twenty feet as we get closer and closer to the front. "Ah, 1996. The glory days. Back when corporations still kept secrets and sold them via the government as an upgrade to the masses. Fools." Faheem rolls his eyes so hard I can almost hear them pop over all the ringing in my head. "Guess they really were as dumb as they looked in their low-hung pants with undies sticking out and light-up shoes."

Maybe the green powder here isn't so bad, and Mary, did you know? "Yes. I know," I say and run my tongue along my upper teeth. "Light-up shoes? What were they thinking? Idiots. Eating modified crops that made its own insecticide and wearing pants like that, determined to trip themselves over. How could anyone think that might turn out okay?" *The dumb are just dumb. Mary, did you know?* "Dude, the song is back," I say before I realize how bizarre that will sound to Faheem, both my partner in crime and enemy while we play chess.

"The song?" He turns around, and one of his huge black eyebrows points up like an arrow planning to take out the sun in one fell swoop.

"Never mind. Guess I can be as dumb as I look, too."

"Gag, you, my Cinnamon man, have never looked dumb."

"Thanks, I think," I say and hope he forgets all about the song in my head because we both know he is not as smart as I am by about five IQ points and that songs were outlawed decades ago to prevent negative associations between music and behavior. I wonder what genius made up that rule. "Forget about it," I say in my best Brooklyn accent.

"Forget what?" he asks, and there goes that magazine-worthy brow of his again.

"Forget about it." I double down on the accent. But he just looks confused, like someone who never heard of Brooklyn. Or old cop movies. Or just forgot all about Barbra and her nose.

So I give up and try to find solace somewhere else. Behind me maybe? I start to turn around, but something deep inside tells me not to, that something behind me is just too big to look at when I'm hurting like this. *Forget about it.* Instead, I look side to side, realizing our lines have come close enough together that I can read the name tags of some of the AIPs in the lines next to us. Some of them I have met but not more than a handful. I count eight lines converging into each small grouping. I've actually seen the pods from an aerial view, so I know there are eight units inside each larger unit that is constructed on a steel platform in the shape of an octagon—like a massive stop sign. *Stop. Stop what?*

As we laugh and walk the rest of the way to drop, I realize I don't actually know much about what happened after the GMOs and ridiculous pants. No one really does. It was such a whirlwind according to the online pre-Grid history programs. Just that national autism rates, especially in fair-skinned boys, skyrocketed along with severe allergies, especially in darker-skinned children. And…so many kids died that we are missing an entire generation of AIPs—some by the escalating diseases, others at their own hand after they became infected with some poisoning by a process called "social media" that made them want to die. I'd love to say I understand what "social media" was, but all records of its existence have been wiped off the mainframes of the Grid so it can, and I quote here, *"Never happen again."*

Each ethnic or social group, it seemed, had its own unique malignant process designed…just for them. Like an entire population, crippled in a matter of years. Massive cancer rates in middle-aged adults arose. Rare diseases of childhood became common again. Measles killed thousands. Some rare influenza spells incapacitated third world countries. The plague resurfaced. Suicides skyrocketed. And in one massive movement fueled by some women doctors on a website that disappeared off the records along with an explanation of a "social media" platform name Lookbook, the entire food and medical supply systems were overhauled. All of it happened seemingly overnight by the first biohackers who, under the authority of Vantage CEOs, had the power to do so. *What is a lookbook? A book of faces? A book of blank eyes?*

It's all we know. Before that time, no one seems to remember anything. Amazing, Inc. infiltrated the food and product distribution industry by offering unparalleled delivery speed. One major insurance company named Kaiper Longevity took over healthcare. Another education, etc. The best stood up and accepted their exclusive Vantage contracts in the Grid and ignored the rest of the floundering world. Lucky bastards. Within a few short years, everything changed. Well, for those who stayed anyway. For those who signed their membership agreements without so much as pausing to read the fine print like me. For those who had something to offer the group yet were willing to be isolated in their particular fields of contribution for mass benefit. The rest, those without skills or unwilling to place all their faith in the hands of Vantage—who knows what happened to them.

I take a deep breath and give thanks for being a member of the Grid and return to my conversation with my best friend in the whole wide Grid. "G, I do so love you."

"Kiss my grits," he says and tries not to laugh at the absurdity of his words. "Back at you."

"Also, that was an old expression. Kiss my grits. TV show, I think. Sitcom about a woman who gave up her dreams of becoming a dancer or singer or something to work in a craphole diner in Phoenix. Alice, both her and the program's name. But the grits belonged to another character. Swirl? Surge? What was her name?"

He shrugs his shoulders. "This Mr. Massy with two Ss doesn't have a clue. Why do you know so much about old television programs? They are long gone and not coming back, buddy. Just like diners. I bet they served grease on grease there. I could go for some grease. Screw wheatgrass."

The ringing in my ears increases, and I remember the name. "Flo. Her name was Flo. And I love wheatgrass. What's wrong with you? You probably miss donuts too, Mr. Massy." We both snap at the same time. *My ass.*

"Clever name—Flo. I like the swirling sound of that. And donuts, I like the sound of that even more." He smiles before he puts his hand over his mouth, makes a kissing motion, and directs the kiss toward my backside. "Phoenix. That's in old Arizona, right? Watershed zone, even. Poor diner."

"Yes. Watershed. Almost completely off the Grid but not exactly. And thanks," I say, feeling better by the minute. No more seeing stars. No more discussing the pesticide-producing-corn pre-Grid days. My friend is back for reals. And the ringing keeps getting quieter and quieter the closer we get to our destination despite missing grease and pastries and television. That's good.

"Ecomewl." *Welcome.* His fingers click.

Now my fingers. "Fine. Fine, Ham." I suddenly remember it really was his turn to go first tonight. "Sorry, Dude. I was being a kid, add c." *Dick.*

"Even-steven after that punch. My bad. Some nights I just get so…I don't know…anxious right before we drop." He reaches out his arms and spins a circle, looking up at the sky, and his fingers come four feet from touching the rails of the next group over. So close now.

I take a breath and hope it will all be okay…but part of me is not so sure that Vantage designed this place as well as everyone thinks they did. "Ditto. It's okay. Other than the ringing in my ears and song now looping for all eternity in my mind, I'm fine." I wink like I'm kidding, but I am not. *Mary, did you know?*

"What song?" We both laugh, but his grin works up his cheekbones and takes over his eyes because he means it.

Mine stays right around the corners of my mouth because that is what fake smiles do while you are lying—they stick. I'll try to remember that...how a real smile spreads but a fake one just sticks there under a table like gum no one wants to chew anymore.

As I ponder all the gum under all the tables in all the desolate diners in places like Phoenix that probably have been abandoned for decades now, I sweep my gaze across the lines and lines of us heading in for the night and calculate how many of us have been granted security clearance to use this mega station for sleep. *The blind. Mary, did you know?*

Eight times eight times eight pairs of us. Like eight stop signs to the third, even fourth power. *Stop. Stop what?* One thousand and twenty-four of the highest-ranked workers in this Vantage city division. I can't pretend to know the ranking of the other seven sections on this mainframe because what I know is all I am allowed to know. But we are the highest ranked grouping that I make assignments to...all of us lucky enough to have a skill set that uniquely employs our higher human mind —innate skill potentials that cannot be totally automated by our advanced machinery and thus requires sleep—the ultimate luxury. Screw disgust. I prefer the luxury of sleep. Twenty-three words inside sleep. Sleep. Sleep. Even the letters feel like fine linen, shimmer like silk, and are more precious than diamonds. S.L.E.E.P—my favorite five letters. *The dumb. Mary, did you know?*

Thankfully, all of us AIPs also earn enough V-bucks to be able to afford access to nightly sleep programs. I think about working all night without any sleep breaks, and my nausea multiplies. No sleep—ultimate poverty. The idea, awful. Just awful. Like a computer game division without a chess program. Awful. Intolerable. A total waste of time.

Now I can't help but notice all the containment chambers in front of us are arranged like the screens we use for playing Infinity Chess War. Eight across by eight down, alternating black and white. We plug in the two AIPs in front of us—Aston and Santo. Then it's our turn, and the two behind us plug us in. I can't help but wonder who plugs in the last two guys in the last unit. Must suck being those monkeys. But who cares. It's not me, so why should I worry about anybody else? In this life, all I can afford to care about is being better tomorrow at my work than I was today, my occupational and therefore dormancy partner, and the two girls behind us who hook us in. That's it. Well, and handing over my eternal loyalty to Vantage. Whoever that is. Simple price to lead a simple but ultimately perfect life here in the Grid.

"It's the week before Christmas you know, Ham," I yell as we both load the guys up before us and close the volcanic rock door to their station. He engages the six-foot-tall Himalayan salt lamp on the right, and I activate the one on the left.

He just shakes his head. "Name's Faheem. How could I ever forget Christmas, Gag? Best day of the year. Although what's up with the man in the red suit and snow. Snow was terrible. Thank G for climate control."

"You could be a little more generous and a little less stingy this week. Like let me go first, you know. I think Christmas used to be about giving to the needy or some ancient concept like sharing your good fortune." My turn to blow the kiss his way. If I turned around, my fingers would touch the girl in the line next to me. I lock eyes with her, glance at her nametag–Elida, and then look back into her eyes that are missing some-thing. Something beautiful that I have no name for. Purpose maybe? Joy maybe? Only the need within her empty eyes remains. *What is a lookbook? A book of faces? A book of blank eyes?*

"Needy? We have no needy. Remember? Besides, there is no such thing as good luck, my man. Only working hard enough to reach your genetic and biological potential. Everyone knows that." He struts, lifting up each of his shoulders in the dance of anticipation for what comes next. Our turn comes. He whispers, "Yes," and licks his lips.

We both walk around to our station and wave at the two girls behind us. Lacie and Celia. Both are Supporters, subclass SW—Social Workers. I think they lead the team who manages the misfits messing up the grand plan of our ideal city. Lacie waves briefly but then turns her attention back to her partner who just shifts back and forth, staring at her own two feet. Seems like Lacie is always taking care of that girl. Shame. I wish she talked to us more.

"Fair is fair, Gag," he says, puts his EMF protection medallion around his neck, presses his finger to the pad for payment, and quickly climbs into his pod to drop in first.

"Second drop isn't so bad, Ham." His nap pod door closes, and I hear the device engage. Despite the thick window, I see the nightlight around his head intensify and know he's gone. Far away in some virtual reality experience while he sleeps. *My turn. Dropping is what matters. It's all that matters. That, I bet, every Mary knows.*

I yawn, and my mouth waters slightly, getting ready to pick my travels for the night. After about a minute, I try to yawn again to speed up my drop, but for some reason, I can't hold on to the air long enough, and my stomach flips like I just made the wrong move playing chess and can't take my piece back. Pressing the button for "Romance" as tonight's reality sleep program of choice, I feel a bit better again and take three deep breaths. Another few moments pass—nothing. My stomach clenches. The taste of metal floods my mouth, and my heart races. That's when I realize I'm still not asleep. For the first night in as long as I can remember, I am not asleep. And this... this virtual reality love affair might just be a horror film.

Chapter Two

LEANING BACK into my grey seat, enjoying the spongy foam and leather hybrid cradling my non-sleeping body, I look around my soundproof chamber and, for the first time ever, really look at this dormancy space where I normally sleep. With sleep abnormally evading me, I look up at the underside of a curved layer of plastic and glass with little flashing lights that resembles the inside of what an egg might, I suppose. The whole space I'm in is mostly taken up by the chair and its two armrests. The chamber, best I can guess, probably measures about two by one by two meters, just enough space for me to roll from one side to the other and back, so I do. I lie here for a few minutes considering that maybe the system is uploading a new program and will kick in. Maybe. I mean, I paid my fee, right? Maybe I am out of V-bucks? Is that even possible?

I roll to my other side and notice that the chair's material immediately accommodates me in its conforming foam, and I relax a bit. My eyes wander up and down the polished silver walls, looking for something to focus on other than my discomfort. The seams that connect the inner panels are fine and smooth, each corner marked only by a cluster of eight small dots. As annoyed as I am that my program hasn't started, I am glad that the designer of these things must have valued the number eight as much as I do. Maybe I am out of Vantage bucks. Maybe?

I check my account balances—general, savings, emergency, and retirement—quickly by pressing my finger to my wrist. Nope. All accounts full. Maybe something else is happening. Maybe Mary knows what is wrong? *Who is Mary?*

By habit, I start with all five letters of the word "maybe" and go down from there while I look around my pod. *Maybe: beamy, embay.* The seats in the pods are really insanely comfortable. Well designed. Beautiful. Functional. Maybe the best possible version... *Maybe: beam, mabe, abye, bema.* There's a subtle ventilation grate close to the floor's edge that I've never noticed before. *How clever.* The air coming in has a slightly sweet lavender-like scent to it and feels cool and wonderful on my face. Must be some sort of essential oil. *Maybe: aby, aye, bam, bey, bye, yea, yam.* Several controls and monitors seem to be tracking data of some sort. Vitals or similar, I guess. *Maybe: ab, ae, am, ay, ba, by, em, ma, me, my, ya, ye.*

There sure are a lot of words inside "maybe." Thirty-four, to be exact. I like exact. And...thirty-four, the same number as years I am old, at least. Maybe I missed a few. If Faheem were here, he would have asked me, *"Missed a few words or years, Bro?"*

And for once, I wouldn't be able to decide which answer made the most sense.

My hands run up and down the seat for some indeterminate amount of time while I think about some of my favorite words and all the words inside of them. After what must be a few hours, I start an imaginary game of chess in my mind and replay a few of my most brilliant moves against Faheem, trying to make that dang song stop playing. I anagram him for the millionth time. *Faheem: fehme, heame, ahem, fame, hame, heme, fee, ham, meh.* There are thirty-seven words in Faheem. The best as far as I am concerned is "ham." I laugh because he would say the best word inside his name is "fame."

To exercise my fingers, I do the motions of the alphabet in sign language but can't form the proper movements because my hands shake too much, and I give up. The song has been replaced by the prime numbers I keep listing in a sequence to soothe myself—*2, 3, 5, 7, 11, 13, 17, 19*... I get up to 97 in my list and then count them in the opposite direction, hoping that will help—97, 89, 83, 79, 73, 71, 67, 61. But it doesn't. Factorials next—0! is 1, 1! is 1, 2! is 2, 3! is 6, 4! is 24, 5! is 120, 6! is 720, 7! is 5,040, 8! is 40,320. Still no relief.

I keep going over and over what went wrong but get lost in the swirl of my erratic thoughts. Never can I remember feeling this disorganized, this unstable. But then again, I can't remember not sleeping either.

Massaging my temples, I try to ease my pounding head but can't stop shaking it. I feel anxious but am too tired to figure out why and sink back into my foam seat. Math can solve anything. Need more math. Again the prime numbers. Forward, backward. Factorials forward, backward. Then square numbers next. "One, four, nine, sixteen," I whisper but can't seem to get past eighty-eight times itself. How is that even possible? My last IQ test, I scored one hundred and forty-seven. *Help me, eight. Eight, you always save me. Where are you? Stop. Save me. Save us all, eight.*

My legs cramp, and I want to stretch them, but I can hardly lift my leg up against gravity and just let the cramps take over. Eventually, they pass after what could be eight or eighty-eight minutes. But not the twisting in my guts, which never stops.

Growling, I am so irritable I seriously consider punching

myself in the face. But I can't concentrate enough to form a fist to do it or carry out the steps or think about the words inside the word "punch."

Finally, a subtle vibration begins from within my seat, and I realize it is almost the time I normally wake up...like wake up for the day. Today—six days before Christmas. Holy hell. More than six hours have already passed, and honestly, I remember only minutes here and there of pain. Insane.

Trying to gather myself adequately before the nap pod opens and I have to somehow find myself enough to make it through today, I think about my own name—Jagga. I know it means something. *Mary, did you know?* But I guess neither Mary nor I can remember what right now. I am just too sleepy, too tired. *Who are you, Mary? Who is your son?*

Counting the nine words out loud, I say, "Gaga, jaga, jagg, aga, gag, jag, aa, ag, and ja. There are nine words inside of me. Nine. Nine. I am nine. I am." *But I wish I was eight. Eight, the only perfect number.*

Faheem, who has always been so much wordier than me (thirty-seven vs nine), knocks on my pod, and the door opens. He laughs. "O. M. G. *Best Day Ever*. So love that program. I got this new girl in *Best Day Ever* this time. She. O. M. G. Dude. Just. Dude." Then he blinks his eyes rapidly and shakes his head so fast back and forth like the bobblehead doll on our desk and laughs like no person should. I'd worry what's wrong with him usually, but right now, I'm only worried about me, so I just roll my eyes.

"You're all jelly today, Gag, and we just got started. Dude. I mean. Dude."

I clench my teeth and stretch my neck. "Dude, please stop the mini sentences for effect shit. I hate it when you do that. Help me up, Ham. Seriously. I'm in pain over here."

"Pain? Did you just say...?" He rolls the word around on the tip of his tongue and finally spits it out. "Tish? Oh, snap!"

"No. I said 'shit,' not 'tish.' You recall the word, the concept. Pain, you've heard of it too, I'm sure. I mean it. Help me."

"K. And don't bug on me for that one. K is a sentence of its own. It just is. K?" he commands more than asks and bobbles his head again like he's trying to clear it or something. "What program did you run last night to give you...pain?"

I just groan.

"Do we even have pain? Is that an option? Can I try it? Tell me more." He smirk-smiles.

"Nothing. K. At. All," I mock him. He laughs because he probably thinks I am trying to be funny. He also probably thinks I had some reality experience of unparalleled intensity. This time, he'd be wrong. Squared. Nothing times nothing, still nothing.

"Fine. Don't share," he says and shows off an old dance we used to do called flossing. "I won't either. Not a word about her red, wavy dress and her ripped thighs and how she wrapped..." I put one of my green bean fingers to my lips and stop his periodic hip and switching arm thrusts right there. He groans, doing one last floss before he reaches into my pod and uses the strength of his brisket-thick arms to pull me out like a piece of broccoli stuck between his massive teeth.

I groan back. Thankfully, my legs don't cramp up too hard, and I can actually stand—stand enough to get out of my pod before I realize how badly my stomach hurts.

"Fine. Suit yourself." He skips away, and now all I see is his rump roast getting farther and farther away from me while I try not to shit my pants right there like what's-his-name in that old movie about heroin abuse—that shocking scene they use in annual Vantage membership training to teach us about the horrors of unregulated heroin use in the boredom-ridden days of old. A film called *Trainspotting*. Now they have perfected its use. Kept the good parts, minimized the bad, and trained the Heroin Medicals to dispense it periodically to the fully integrated AIPs to maximize their efficiency.

From this point forward, I decide the word "shit" and "train" shall be as interchangeable in my vast vocabulary as all my beloved anagrams.

Thankfully, I make it to the toilet in time. Unlike junk-boy in the film, I don't dive in.

Chapter Three

WE DO our work for the day, evaluating the occupational potential of hundreds of youth, and it's fair to say I function at a level less than optimal, my ineptitude akin to ultimate failure in our realm. Vantage has two perspectives of an individual's evaluation in the Grid—perfect or fail. That's all we get. An A plus or an F—which is as good as dead—from the corporation. What a bunch of assholes. That's it. No second chances. Ever. I take a second shot of Shatterproof coffee and hope it will help, but it doesn't. Who am I kidding?

I would love to make some clever joke right now, but let's face it…cleverness and personal comfort are as inversely proportional as supply and demand in a capitalistic economy. Every novice in economics knows that.

Another shot. Still, no better. Minutely hopeful despite my grave and dwindling prognosis in the humor department, I try an extra teaspoon of omegas. I will probably just end up *training* in the toilet four times today instead of three.

"Did you skip a colonic this cycle or something? Miss a plant powder, maybe?" Faheem asks after I visit the bathroom and mess up both the toilet and our schedule for the second time this shift. "The last error you made was a year ago. You are always perfect and always expect perfect in other people. Dang. Two errors in one afternoon. Dude, you okay? Or is pain just that good? I could skip *Best Day Ever* for—"

"Perfection," I cut in, the urge to correct his grammar undeniable.

"My point exactly. So are you okay or not?"

"Nope. I'm. Not," I say, using his own best vocabulary trick against him. I'd lie, but why bother? I've used up all the gum under this dinner table and can't even waste the energy to plaster fake smiles to my less-than-attractive face. Maybe an ugly expression suits my ugly features better anyway. Maybe. Thirty-four words for my thirty-four years. Maybe.

"K. Getting. Worried. About. You. Bro. Now. Laugh. For. G's. Sake."

G's sake. What's G? Oh yeah, that Christmas dude. No, wait. That's Santa. Or is it? Mary, did you know? I make the most pathetic fake laugh ever, and my lips stay as straight and flat as the x-axis on a graph that goes on forever like the digits in pi.

To make up for the holes in my register, Faheem quickly evaluates a second-grader named Jay as destined to play as a high-level fütballer in the entertainment department.

Sighing, I say, "Well. Sort of." I can't speak for my occupational partner, but I consider my two-word sentence an improvement in my mental status despite the fact that it's incomplete and so far from perfect and get almost hopeful. Almost.

That kid, Jay the fütballer, walks away from us, and I can't help but notice how flawlessly the child balances both his legs and arms without an ounce of cockiness. We've run him through multiple scenarios—offense, defense, unsolvable, flawed plays, balls that according to our algorithms are impos-

sible to catch, a defect in the floor under his feet, missing team-
mates, coaches calling the wrong plays. He outsmarts them all.
He doesn't claim the virtual playing field we drop him in. He is
the freaking field.

"Wait," I shout. "Take him back and relevel him." *Six
words. Complete thought. No grammatical errors. Massive
improvement.* I keep going. "Not fútball like in England. Football like in Texas during *Friday Night Lights.* Football, quarter-
back maybe." *Maybe. Thirty-four possibilities.*

Ham's eyebrow shoots up like two sides of an equilateral
triangle.

"Dude, did you see how he balanced his arms?" I smile for
real now. "Not high level. Champion level. Tish, not champion
level." *Shit.* The smile spreads to my sleepy eyes, and they
wake up. "Champion coach level possibly. Intelligence oozes
from that kid. That kid and the field are one. He will take the
sport to a whole new level. Maybe invent a new game. Call it
Infinity Ball or something."

Faheem claps. "There you are, my man. Welcome back to
the best of them. I was so, so missing my B.F.F! You have
Person Planning in your blood, Bro. No wonder you run this
department—"

"We run this—"

He laughs. "Whatever. Dude. You. Have. No. Idea," he says
and rolls his eyes despite his smile. "You are right about that
kid. You're always right. I see it now...that kid's future.
Inevitable. Brilliant."

I start humming an old Vantage slogan and sway from side
to side, which is as close to flossing as my dance skills will ever
come. *"Don't worry, sit tight. The might of Vantage is always
right."*

Another boy comes next. He sits down, plugs into the white
testing pod, and waits while the straps engage his hands,

making sure he can't move once we get started. I can't help but notice he appears older than his reported DOB. Like he skipped the end of the mass annihilation of Generation Z only to suffer precocious puberty and became his own anatomically superior cohort. Generation A2 perhaps? I stare at him. Eleven as per my report but closer in size and development to fifteen or sixteen. Beginnings of a beard shadow, bulging genitalia, high forehead, muscular arms that hang lower than I would expect, and a unique birthmark on his arm. Blood red, it almost looks like the letter "T." Or maybe an "F." The mark reminds me of something. A song perhaps. No, an idea.

A few virtual reality programs flash in front of him. By the length and nature of his gaze at certain images, we can infer his natural talents, attractions, vibrations. Within a few seconds, I notice he doesn't really notice anything. Like he's eternally stuck where I was a few minutes ago—lost in the no-land doing no-thing but no-thing. The only unifying theme in his response to the images, colors, and patterns is the kind of absence an artificially intelligent robot might have in the feelings department. So, as my program instructs, I shoot up an image of a mouse dying, writhing around as if in pain. Finally, the system gets a hit from his autonomic nervous system on my monitor, the screens of which go absolutely wild with data. More images. More responses. As the stronger hits come, the program fine-tunes the stimulation to see what images evoke the greatest responses from the kid.

I read his rap sheet. Healthy, normal, both parents actively employed in the Grid, serving as contributing members of society. Psychopath, not sociopath, is what the DSM would have labeled him years ago. Apparently, this one was born this way.

Most people in the old days didn't realize some deviants don't have to be made. They just…are. Thank G for our modeling programs.

Baffled at how rare a specimen he must be, I stand there unable to calculate his potential occupations for a moment. Then I realize there aren't many. Aren't many…is an exaggeration. None, other than criminal activity, is more accurate. In the old days, it would have taken an exhaustive middle school evaluation, some failed high school relationships, a diagnosis of antisocial personality disorder, fights, lack of response to the usual meds, some wet bedsheets, a few dead animals, detention, drug trafficking, maybe a prison sentence for killing a few hundred idiots attending an outdoor country music concert for us to make the conclusion that he's a big fat zero. Now we can almost perfectly predict his future in moments by pairing images on a screen—smells, sounds, etc.—and the subsequent areas that light up on his brain scan. That and a quick biome evaluation and basic DNA scan, of course.

Thanks to the biohackers, we know how far a particular human has to excel. Or in this case, not excel at anything that serves the common good other than military service. I recall one of my original training pearls: "Psychopaths made great snipers when we the government still utilized people for such violent acts"…or so the Vantage program stated. I try to locate that section in my updated manual to confirm the memory is accurate but can't. I guess since we no longer have violence, we no longer need snipers. Section deleted. Efficient of Manual Writers. Guess the last few I…I mean we…assigned are doing a good job.

When we started assigning status potential this way, it used to bother me, but not anymore. The void boy is who he is—genetically, neurologically, bacterially colonized at birth. Not my fault. I'm not cold about it. Just a realist. "Washer, biohazard tubes."

Faheem mutters something under his breath, and I wonder if it is from boredom or disagreement.

"No sleep required," I add. "Full isolation from all other persons of all classes due to a complete lack of empathy."

Faheem raises his eyebrow but says nothing.

"This one for full integration. Insert a heroin PICC line. He requires and deserves no higher mind functions," I say into my recorder machine and enter the proper codes and written orders.

To confirm, I place my right thumb on the thumb pad at the base of my center screen. Faheem swallows hard and then places his left thumb next to mine to authenticate my confirmation as validated by two informed sources.

Immediately, the solution running the IV attached to the boy's hand changes colors. He is whisked away, more sedated than alert, to an integration processing site where they will do whatever it is they do to upgrade his mind. Then to the PICC line teams and, finally, off to his work site.

Again, not my fault. But for a second or two, I get lost in thinking about what makes us unique. What makes me—me the master of veggies and anagrams. Faheem—the king of meat slabs, chess, and the second best anagramer around with a slightly lower IQ than mine. But then I remember the more time I spend thinking about what I am doing, the less time I will have to actually do it, so I get on with my day. Faheem seems to avoid making eye contact with me, and I assume it must be because I made so many mistakes this morning. Paybacks suck.

Three more assignments file in to be evaluated by the Vantage program and its two elite Person Planners. Our program is almost perfect. Almost. Apparently, it lacks one thing. No one has a word for it that fits more perfectly than "intuition." It's what Ham-It-Up and I have that almost every human and all robots do not. A sense. A sixth sense actually. A feeling. An unexplainable certainty about the nature of another human. I guess that is why they still need the two of us to run our division. If they didn't, maybe Faheem and I would live more like birth-mark boy than kings of the imaginary chicks in *Best Day Ever*.

Back to the task at hand. We stare at our screen, built, I imagine, much like a massive eight foot across and high two-way mirror might be, and watch the three who come next. One at a time, two females and one male appear before us. They sit down, strap in their seats, and while looking first in our direction, they face their screens. After they respond to a few images, we spin their chairs around and watch their screens and paired brain scan images making various connections on how their brains work.

This odd feeling of déjà vu courses through me. Chills down my chicken skin. The room the kids are in seems so familiar even though I don't know that I have actually been there in person. They must be in the Grid. But where? How far? How close? The next room maybe? *Thirty-four possibilities*. But I can't say for sure because our screen is dark before they come and after they go.

We make a few additional observations, change the images accordingly, simultaneously analyze their biome and DNA data, and narrow down their options. Sometimes it's fast. Sometimes not so fast. Each case is a new case.

For these three—librarian for general searches, grand architect in mass housing projects, and low-level security prison cook. Like a miracle, we've finished our assigned intakes three minutes before the day's ending bell. Only sixteen hours at work today. Thank G it was a short one today because I am so dang tired.

Faheem rubs his hands and steps back from our adjustable eco and ergonomically friendly desk, probably six feet long, that allows for comfortable sitting or standing with the press of a button. I roll my neck and rub my right shoulder.

"I am spending those three extra minutes with her tonight in *Best Day Ever*." He grins.

Yesterday we finished two minutes early, so much like Faheem, I consider this three-minute finish, despite my poor attitude, great progress. Until I look at the screen on my left wrist and realize those three minutes of extra sleep will mean absolutely nothing to me tonight. Tomorrow will surely be even worse. Normally, I would look at my V-buck balance after today's work. But why bother? What can I spend the money on now?

I grunt while my annoying partner saunters across the low-pile carpet made from old recycled plastic bottles, performing some less-than-sexy dance move he calls the Roger Rabbit that...let's face it...much like counting with an abacus, needs to be wiped from his memory bank. His flossing moves suck like an equation I can't solve without writing it on paper...but not nearly as much as this rabbit shit that even Stephen Hawking couldn't have solved with a thousand computers and his perfect mind before he died all those years ago.

"What. Is. Up. Your—?" He jerks his dance backward to the rhythm of his mini sentences.

I cut him off. "Tub—add t?" *Butt.* "Nothing but nothing."

He stops all the bunny moves. "Is that a joke? Sorry I missed it. I am so...thinking about her." He smiles, and this time it spreads beyond his eyes and right up to the top of his head.

To spite him, I refuse to ask any questions about my occupational partner's new lover. Fake lover. She isn't real. Their affair isn't real. None of this is real. It's pretty much just a fake piece of ass in a fake world.

I hear a beeping alarm and turn around to gather the two pill cups that have just materialized on the corner table near the exit door. I pick up both small glass containers, which signals the exit door to our control station to open.

Faheem takes his from me and swallows them in one swift motion and does a little leap in the air. "Dude. Let's go already."

But I'm frozen, wasting at least one of our precious minutes. I stare hard at my two blue pills like decoding lasers will shoot out of my eyes and tell what's really in them. No such luck. Twirling my assigned supplements between my fingers, I wonder…are they real? Am I real? Is my life real? Or am I just some fake piece of ass too? Some zero, some code in some reality program in Stephen Hawking's ancient computer? Heck, maybe I'm the computer. Maybe the Matrix in that old movie was real, and all of this is fake. I decide to take the blue mystery pills anyway because my buddy is already out the door and heading to the electronic walkway that leads to the central tram. I can't afford to lose him, and he is obviously not waiting for me.

"Wait," I holler and try to catch up while not thinking about pill colors and old movies and things I somehow couldn't remember before yesterday—before my head started ringing.

I make it to the tram and catch Faheem's hand before the door closes. As he pulls me in, just in time, the image of the two blue pills returns, and I sigh.

He just laughs. "Best pills ever get us into the *Best Day Ever*. Or is it night?"

I look round. There are so many of us on the tram, and we all look almost the same in our hooded uniforms, the differing hues almost lost to the dullness of each shade. To block my train of thought, I say, "Best math ever," and consider the properties of multiples and zeros instead of my insignificance as we file away from our filling stations and head toward dormancy in the nap pods. Or at least they do. Not me. Nope.

The certainty of a basic math principal soothes me almost as much as calculating anagrams or counting in prime numbers, so I give it my best and drop into my math because I'm pretty sure I won't be dropping into dormancy tonight.

1. Anything multiplied by zero is zero. *All the time in the world and no time for sleep for me. Maybe time isn't real. Maybe sleep isn't real.*

2. Any number divided by itself is one. *We are all truly alone. In the end, you live and die by yourself— utterly alone. Nothing you do really matters. I've never mattered.*

3. Any number divided by zero is undefined. *Anything should be possible, so why isn't that true? Life isn't like math, is it? One day that fact will be the root of the ultimate revolution. Revolutions are more like an old Indie film than good math. Unpredictable. Layered. Complex. Poorly understood. Illogical and risky. Financially unsustainable.*

This shit-train of thought really isn't that much better after all. We step off the tram and keep going. "What is zero divided by zero?" I ask, more myself than Mr. Ham Face all focused on his now two extra minutes with what's-her-name's ripped thighs and red wavy skirt…which aren't real.

"One." He smiles, all enraptured with his own cleverness as we glide through more sliding doors, move from one building into another, and receive the next level of treatments.

"No, indeterminate, I think." I squint and bite my lower lip as I walk through a misting station that decontaminates all undesired bacteria from our hands.

"You think too much," he says and swallows air so he can make a fake burp.

"You're disgusting," I say and he burps again. I sigh hard, blowing my air out like I don't need it anymore. "If A is B times C, then A divided by B is C. But zero is equal to zero times any number. Any number whatsoever. Thus, zero divided by zero is any number whatsoever. And she isn't real. Like you get that, right? Imaginary pussy isn't pussy. It's a computer program."

More swallows. Another burp. "I guess you need to clarify the 'whatsoever,' then. Like you get that, right? Because imaginary math isn't math. It's a desperate attempt to make me feel stupid. Also, it's not working." He does some exercise to activate his psoas muscles while we receive our wheatgrass shots, and I can't help but remember that people used to eat psoas muscles and called it a luxury meat. Filet mignon.

Then I think about that youth—the one who will become the washer with full access to complete automation programs but never truly experience sleep again. Why? Because they don't need his destined-for-failure higher mind here at Vantage, only his body to complete some task critical to survival for the entire Grid. He's important, so important even if his potential is average or, in this case, far less valuable than that. Lucky SOB —easy peasy lemon squeezy life for him even though in the old days, he would have probably become a serial killer and spent his last decades doing hard time, assuming they caught him.

All the while, the other boy will live a long, mentally optimized life because he needs his human mind. All the supplements. All the critical room vibrations, recalibrations, oils, soaps, toxin-free cleansers, and enough sleep to play out every possible scenario between the thighs of the best babes in *Best Day Ever*. Quickly I do the math: 6 hours a night for 90 plus years of playing and then 50 or so years of retirement. That's

328,500 hours of sleep. Why? Because of his ability to throw a ball in some way that a computer can never replicate. Some way that only human hands can perfectly position themselves to toss a ball while taking into consideration too many things to list—things I can't possibly understand even though I know that youth already does...does in his blood. Like...adjusting for the slope of the fields, the mechanics of how he and only he throws, the way his particular receiver catches, the speed of the defensive players coming toward him, the tilt of the planet, effects of the wind blowing, the time of the day. Variables he can't even name. Things that only a human protégé can process and integrate instantly, effortlessly without any program at all. In fact, the programs hurt more than help him...so he goes without them. The bad news is that means he needs sleep. The good news is that he will be able to afford it.

I guess that's the good news anyway. Who can really say?

As biohacking evolved, we as a utopian society in the Grid became acutely aware that there are only a few things that humans and only humans can do perfectly—things that cannot be automated with ultimate efficiency that our bodies now run. That boy has one of them. I have another. One of the "great gifts," which as far as I am concerned require the most self-sacrifice to possess. One of the innate reasons to be classed as a privileged but terribly burdened Artificially Integrated Person or AIP of Vantage. We are the educators, caregivers, programmers, medicals, artists, and entertainers. We are As in A(d)Vantage. The others...they are just here getting off easy in this place where food, shelter, and resources are all guarantees of your membership in the group. Just another brick easily and efficiently plugged into the wall of the healthy, long life that Vantage offers us. The same corporation into which we place all our faith, all our value, and thus all our worship. *Mary, did you know?*

Chapter Four

THE NEXT TWO days pass without much difference. No sleep. The aches and pain of losing something critical to my body, something my cells need desperately to function. Sleep. *Peels, eels, pees, seep, les, see.* Twenty-three words, getting less and less tolerable by the night, by the hours within each night. *Eel, sel, pe.*

I go from one line to the next—line up for my pod, line to my work, line for my plant powders, line for my green drinks, my Shatterproof coffee. Repeat.

My nightlight is still not connecting in and uploading to my nap pod, and I have nowhere to turn for help at this point. Yesterday, I found an excuse to go to the Sleep Program Department and take a look around. I hinted to the pair of AIPs who update the hardware for the servers that some of our night-lights might need an upgrade. I trust them minimally at best and couldn't safely give them any more details after I saw their dropped jaws and open mouths after suggesting we might need updates or small, hardly significant alterations in the program.

One of them gasped. "But that program is perfect. Vantage leadership says so. And they are always—"

"Right. Of course they are. I was testing you."

He sighed. "Whew! Almost had me there."

I forced a laugh. "Kidding. Perfect is perfect. Duh. You passed. I'll tell leadership."

The poor kid smiled and gave the other kid a high five while I went on about how great Vantage is because I have noticed in my few days without sleep that no one here ever says anything negative about anything, especially Vantage. They smiled some more and bumped fists before they eventually went happily back to whatever job Faheem and I had assigned them who knew how long ago.

That left me to be the only one in the Grid who thinks negative thoughts about anything. Lucky me, I get to keep them all to myself. I tried to think back to when I got so freaking grumpy, and the ringing in my ears resumed. That sucked, so I stopped thinking about much at all. Then I started looking elsewhere without any more hints to anyone else—searching online and even in the "restricted" section, again under the ruse that I was trying to perfect a portion of my Persons Planning Program to make sure Sleep Programs stayed adequately and fairly staffed.

Turns out even the retired information application Vous-Tube has no videos on the subjects, the great library has no manuals in the historical section, and no other information exists anywhere that I can find it. What I did learn is the functionality of the nightlight device is Vantage proprietary information. No one single named department controls it as far as I can tell. And it also appears that in the very small fine print of our membership agreements...the ones we've all signed with our exclusive contracts, we have exactly twenty-four hours to report any issues with the device, with any device for that matter. But in my opinion, the most interesting thing is a totally-dripping-in-lawyer-terms clause specifically mentioning the nightlight. No other Grid-provided tech has a similar specific mention. Best I can translate the legal jargon…one minute over the limit and we are out of compliance with the "must always function with full disclosure regarding all nightlight usage" clause in our annual agreements signed after watching that terrible video about the *Four Forms of Violence in the Workplace* each year. Not that any of us read this doc. Well, I don't at least. Not until now.

So not telling Vantage, even though I didn't realize what I was doing by that, is considered one of the four forms of *violence* directed toward the corporation and myself. Another old slogan returns to my memory. *"He who omits, Vantage never admits. He who lies, out in the Rustic, is doomed to die."*

By not sleeping, I am now effectively carrying a weapon to work—a weapon made of lies. A weapon that immediately negates my contract to live in the Grid. A weapon that will hurt me far more than it could ever possibly hurt them, I might add. And G knows I like to add.

Surely no one will tell me what to do next because if they don't report my information withholding…my weapon will become their weapon. Pretty much…I am screwed. Heck, even I wouldn't help me if I asked myself. Why would a stranger risk losing so much when there is nothing to gain that they don't already have? Suddenly, I like the concept of subtraction a whole lot less than addition. About as much as Venn diagrams if I am being honest.

I've doubled my Ritalin, tripled my Shatterproof, quadrupled my Ginseng and Kanna. Yet despite my multiplication, I make mistakes, more each day than the one before. By week's end, I will either lose my position as City Person Planner or be forced to surrender to the authorities for keeping a secret—one that divides the everything I used to be into the fraction of an AIP I am now. Who knows what will happen. Will I have a trial? With lawyers and a jury of my peers? How can I when I have only one peer who also happens to be my partner and BFF? An evaluation, then? A reprogramming, maybe? Or will they let it slide for someone as hard to replace as a City Persons Planner? I try to recall an event like this in the past…but I have none. Effectively, a pi without any left of the thirty-four slices. Maybe?

My math jokes and anagrams used to be funny. Used to be. Even I hate them now.

My internal optimist goes a tad wild even though my negativity seems to get the best of me today. Secrets are not allowed, but what about for the elite? Could a punishment for me exist off the chart, previously un-graphed? *Maybe.* Maybe I can trade my V-bucks and buy my way out. *Maybe.*

But as much as I want to think outside the box, thirty-four words inside *maybe* don't get me any closer to an answer no one will tell me until I've already revealed my hand. It's like a game of Infinity Chess War where I have moved my queen, only I can't even see what pieces my opponents are playing on the lowest board with or where the pieces currently stand on a central board. *Checkmate.*

If I had just turned myself in the first night, maybe I would have been okay. Maybe there would have been some answer, some upgrade, some option. Now, not only am I broken in a world that recycles and repurposes anything less than ideal, but I have been withholding information. Effectively lying, which is akin to direct *violence*. The old slogan returns once more. *"He who omits, Vantage never admits. He who lies, out in the Rustic, is doomed to die."*

The punishment for my violent lie, I can only assume— despite the *ass* I make of *u* and *me*—is banishment into the watershed where you have absolutely no guarantees of anything at all. Where only forgotten diners remain with forgotten gum under the tables where no one named Alice or Flo serves grits anymore. Where you must find your own food, own shelter, clothing. Where there are no computers. No programs. No chess games. No pods and no dormancy. No water purifiers. No free electricity. No trams for travel. No supplements—blue or red. No one insuring your safety. No Christmas—the one and only holiday. No lights at night. No antibacterial spray. No ideal biome. No optimized DNA. No prolonged youth. Nothing at all but struggle.

If I don't find a way to fix my own nightlight or function just as well without sleep or convince someone, at their own grave peril, to help me, I am doomed to exile. I think back to how this could have possibly happened, and my ears start ringing again. Like a tsunami from pre-weather control days— waves of angry, negative thoughts assault the shore of my conscious awareness. Then I remember the slap of a thick hand to my back, eight cycles of pain, and that same dang song starts to play on a loop inside my brain again. The lyrics so beautiful and confusing to me drowning out more banished, *violent* curse words than I care to admit. "Oh, that's what happened," I whisper the words just to get them out of my head to make some room for so many other *bad* words trying to take over.

He will have to help me. For Grid's sake, it's his fault. Tomorrow, I will tell Faheem. And if he refuses, then…I will have to make him help me. Whatever that means. *Mary, now we know?*

Chapter Five

TO SAY the following morning with Faheem goes poorly would be as ridiculously minimalist as a Psychiatrist in the days of old telling an overtly suicidal patient to try deep breathing and call him in the morning.

Perhaps that conversation the next day would have gone something like this. The shrink says, *"Oh, why hasn't Annie called? I'll call her. Just check in and see how the breathing went."* The phone rings and rings at Annie's house, but no one answers. The doctor, oblivious to how many Lexapro pills Annie swallowed, hours ago, in fact, goes on about his business of eating some grits for breakfast. *"Probably out taking a walk. I'll try again later."* But there will be no "later" for Annie or walks or more breathing for that matter. Guess therapists needed to be banned for giving out bottles and bottles of pills to people like Annie.

"What...an...idiot," I say, making my words choppy in an accent like my favorite little wizard in a series of movies that for once in the history of ever was as good as the books. If I didn't feel so crappy, I'd wonder where all the books went? And movies, why do we only have Vantage-approved movies now? Who took them? And why? And why can I remember them now but didn't prior to now?

Faheem, probably assuming I mean him and not poor dead Annie's doctor, gets the most aggressive I've seen him in... well, in as long as I can recall. "If you don't stop this insanity now, I will be forced to report you to the safety officer for assaultive negativity in the workplace."

His sausage finger is so close to my mouth that I consider taking a bite and hoping it works as well as bottles and bottles of Lexapro might have. I lick my lips. To avoid my sweeping tongue, he moves his finger sideways under my nose like he wants to keep me from sneezing. But we don't sneeze anymore. No allergens here in Grid means no allergies.

"Have you ever noticed," I add as I love so much to do, "that we work as a pair? Without my thumb, yours is meaning-less." I stick out my left finger and hold it, just under his nose, just like he did. Then I pull the finger back and show it to him. "Minus," I say with a scowling face to convince him how badly my minus sign stinks for us both.

"We cured negativity years ago in the Grid. What. Is. Up. With. You?" He grabs my finger and forces it down so hard it hurts my shoulder and ripples down my back. "Get. Over. Your-self!" Still his chubby digit on his other hand stays close to my mouth even though mine is now back down by my side.

I growl, each word barely escaping my gritted teeth. "Minus. Alone. No. Good. Together. Pair. Better."

"Shut. The. Front. Door. Creep."

I'd tell him how much I hate his mini sentences, but I keep looking at his finger and trying to figure out how he got so big and I stayed so small on the same perfectly tailored Vantage diet. To keep myself from taking a bite, I say, "Duck you. I haven't slept in three days."

"Liar." He rolls his eyes, and his chest shrinks down a bit, but I'll be damned if he doesn't keep that meaty finger right under my nose. I lick again. "Liar. Liar. Liar," he says like somehow it means more the more times he says it. Guess he can add too, but zero plus zero is still zero.

I step slightly forward, because crammed in a corner feels less than pleasant, and try to speak in his terms, this time with open teeth and much less growling. "Not. A. Liar. Dead. Dog. Tired. Can't. Think. Help. Me. I'm. In. Terrible. Pain."

I guess he doesn't believe me because he presses the red panic button with his absurdly thick finger on his grey uniform and waits for the site safety manager to reply. I count the seconds from when he presses the button to when the officer responds. *One.* I never made it to two.

"Hurting. Bad. Real. Dab. Bad. Dab." After I say the "words," I swallow because they are the truest words I have ever spoken. Right now, I am bad forward and backward times four.

Never once breaking eye contact with me, Faheem replies to the officer's monotone and shockingly immediate response. "No, sir. I just hit my body alarm by mistake." He pauses. "Fine. But if I have any concerns... Absolutely. Yep. Immediately. I know. Yes. Vantage has my best interests in mind. Yep." He pauses for a while now. "No, sir. We are right on track to finish our assignments. No problem. We are just fine. You have my word."

Annie's exchange seems so smooth in retrospect compared to this one. At least Annie had a way out. For me, there is none because anything that girls like Annie used to employ to end their overpriced and utterly ineffective counseling sessions with doctors costing three hundred dollars an hour have been taken away. No pills. No ropes. No guns. No razor blades. No syringes. No ingestible poisons. No escape from my pain and the pain I am currently inflicting on pretty much the only person I ever remember having cared about while he threatens to turn me in and hurt me even more than he has already. If I diagrammed that sentence out, the words would almost act like letters in an anagram. The irony makes me laugh but so small that it comes out more like a cough.

After my third night of a nonfunctioning nightlight, I can accept that my negotiating skills are poor and getting poorer by the moment. But honestly, my tolerance to not getting the response I want from Faheem is far poorer. How can he call me partner, buddy, BFF and act like this? Like he's brainwashed into thinking no one ever needs help that Vantage hasn't already offered. Into thinking that in an ideal world with rules set up by a corporation as successful as Vantage that any outliers (especially negative-speaking ones like me) are the problem and not the symptom of a bigger problem. That the outliers are violent and not that violence has been committed against them.

"One more word to me today and I press the button again. For. Reals. Even if both members of our pair go down."

I groan and press the switch that makes my standing desk collapse so I can sit behind it in my silver steel chair. I lay my head down on my arm, and my eyes water like I am going to cry.

"I'll do all of the Persons Planning assignments for both of us today," he says. "All I need is your thumb for confirmation prints. But not another word from you. I. Mean. It."

I transfer the weight of my head over to just my right arm and stick my left hand out to show him that my thumb is all his. My lower lip trembles, but I do not speak, do not argue, do not revolt.

"You. Owe. Me. Big. Time. This is the last day I cover for you." He gets back to work, and I hear him furiously scanning files and trying to catch up for the last ten minutes I have wasted. I can only imagine how many assignments he just made with incomplete information and how those lives will be completely changed because of that. For better? For worse? Who can say? I should care, really care, but I can't be bothered while I'm in this much pain. I flash back to an old Vantage slogan. *"Hurt people, hurt people. With us, you will no longer hurt."* Turns out they were only fifty percent right.

I wonder, getting utterly helpless and hopeless, much like Annie must have, how bad could hell really be compared to this life? No one cares about me. I might as well just top myself and get it over with, but I can't. You think suicidals of old were desperate—imagine suicidal but unable to perform the act. No release. No way out. The ultimate psychological set of blue balls that I can't cut or kill out of me.

A single tear falls down my cheek, but I can't be bothered to wipe it away. That's when the unthinkable happens—the last thing I ever expected to happen. A zero-probability event.

Chapter Six

IF what just happened hadn't happened, I would probably try to explain the next few hours of *My Story, My Life* using a Lagrangian-like approach. That's a physics term. Lagrangian. One of my favorites now that I think about that.

But then again, my explanation would be meaningless outside the context of what just happened. Funny how context matters so much. *"I'll have to remember to remember that. Much like how a fake smile sticks like gum while real smiles spread like waves through the AIP's eyes and up to the forehead,"* I might have whispered. But I can't. Not now.

And I probably would have also laughed because that's funny, the irony so obvious to me in this space even though in linear time it is also meaningless, that I just gave myself some really crucial foreshadowing. And if I can give myself foreshadowing, thus being as clever a reader and anagram solver or Infinity Chess player as I am, I would realize that...*some part of me already knows how this story ends.* Hold on. I need to chew on that little bit of Lagrangian candy for a moment. *Some part of me already knows how this story ends.* Of course, I also couldn't laugh because the idea never would have previously entered my mind in linear time. How could it? Yet here we are...so it must have.

And here as my mind figuratively explodes, I digress even further with another analogy using Infinity Chess War. It's exactly like primitive chess, only you play eight superimposed boards that move in multiple simultaneous directions through space, the pieces moving through multiple boards at once like an old Rubik's cube but far, far more complicated. And thus... far, far more stimulating to math and physics junkies like me.

It's like I am playing a chess match where I see the way out only after the way out is made...thus making my favorite game's name suddenly appropriate for the first time. Infinity Chess War. Names being so important, as if they predetermine the course of events destined to the *named* before the story even gets started—guess the game's name is no different. *Mary, now I know.*

So...before my chess partner plays his particular piece in this imaginary game I make into an analogy to explain how I can explain what just happened to me while it is still happening to me, I'm trapped. Checkmate official on one board—let's just say, the lowest board. And since we are playing boards not only stacked top to bottom but also right to left—eight boards in each direction to be specific—each piece is playing in boards in multiple different directions at the same time. It can get dangerously exciting fast. Why? Often you can't truly understand the implications of a move you are making until you've already made it. But on the lowest board, after eight hours of playing eight boards in eight directions, I'm finally going "down." Not that the direction matters. I was just using an expression, not making a directional statement.

Faheem, who loves to rub it in the few times he actually beats me, makes a move on the top board. He thinks it is funny to draw out my demise, not realizing the chain of events he set in motion. Accidentally, he offers me a possible solution on another board that I wouldn't have even noticed, much like him, if I had been focused just on the lowest board. But I'm not. I'm searching the forest for the trees, while he is trying to burn down my forest by lighting up just one tree. Again, I'm speaking with expressions, not directions. And voilà, a least action principle arrives. Wait, even I am confusing myself. Let me try to explain again with a different approach.

There was a really significant award-winning movie about a short story that elucidated the concept a few years back. Maybe I can use that to help me explain this easier. But only if someone, someone who maybe hasn't even seen the movie, realizes the fundamental flaw with the movie they probably haven't even seen was that understanding an action-limiting principal was crucial to understanding why the plot in the story made sense. Was inevitable, in fact. The inevitability of the ending the whole point of the manuscript to begin with. *Focus, Jagga. Explain better.*

What I am trying to say is that the movie left this one critical concept, the most critical concept actually, out even though the book described it so clearly. So, the movie was flawed intentionally to make it "better" as far as movies are concerned. But that's not my point either. *Shit. Compress the info. Make it easier to understand.*

What I am trying to say is that the ending of the movie was inevitable to begin with. *To begin with. To end with. Is there a difference? Mary, I wish I knew.*

Maybe what happened was inevitable? No. Surely not. How can an impossible and inevitable outcome both be the same outcome? My mind quivers on the edge of a black hole and decides to jump in—much like the time I read that same short story the movie I keep referring to was based on. I remember to remember it now. How could I have forgotten that? A moment in my *now-perception* in linear time when I realized that time, as humanity experiences it, really was an illusionary result of a singular choice—an option we, as descendants of the human race as the story tells it, chose. But not the same option the aliens in the same story selected. The aliens chose to experience life in a Lagrangian-like approach where they already knew all points in linear time and merely played out the sequence of events as they were destined to happen—the idea so clear to them that time is more a filter of experience than a physical reality of how the greater universe operates. In other words, the concept that time isn't real is not just some absurd quantum physics conclusion some professor proposed but the greater truth hidden inside the smaller, faker version of truth we play out like some theatre performance. The shortest, most direct conclusion of the story is that the humans had preferred to participate as actors in the drama while the aliens served as more like the directors of the same play—both perspectives valid as long as the context of the experience was clear. The only problem being that the poor humans didn't know it was just a play. They thought they really were the characters they were playing. Effective, yes, even if quite foolish.

So I remind myself while I flounder at my less-than-perfect description of what is really happening to me in nonlinear "time," that in linear time, my body is still slumped over, resting my head on my left arm on this cold, metal desk while Faheem uses my left thumb to officiate his determinations. Life after life passes before me, but they are not my own, and none of this really matters, so I keep going even though I know I'll fail to explain this well enough until the very end of endings.

Besides, if in a two-hour movie directed by a badass who was paid a fortune to make action-limiting physics obvious enough for the average idiot to comprehend yet no one could, how can I explain it while simultaneously experiencing what just happened to me? I accept that I can't. But I'll do my best because that is the part in this story I am supposed to play. I can only hope my digressions will be forgiven when I finally get where I am going...even though I am also already there.

In the general category of least action principles, the easiest one to explain is from optics, called Fermat's Principle. It holds that light rays moving from one point to another always follow the path that takes the shortest time to travel. In space that is empty, that means a straight line. However, if the same light moves between different media, let's say water...interactions with the water change its speed. This leads to the phenomenon of refraction, which is easily enough for most AIPs, no matter their class, to understand. Fermat's principle of least time gives an AIP another way to think about the path from point A to point B—that light follows and still gets all the same answers even though they are completely different paths.

Impossible yet inevitable, one might think. But not me. I've played enough Infinity Chess War and decoded enough anagrams to know better.

But there are other principles that are far more complicated and far less intuitive to explain that are also based on Lagrangian mechanics where what is minimized is the action, but the basic foundation is the same. And this is the whole plot of that movie summed up in one sentence. I take a breath, both in linear and nonlinear time, and observe the drool running down my right arm. Now it falls off of my elbow and spills onto the desk while Faheem furiously finishes our work for the day like it actually matters.

Here's the whole point of my absurd digression: If you know the state of the system—the story, the movie, the chess game, the life, the history of a society at both the start and end —that system moves from one state to another through whatever sequence of intermediate states minimizes the action. And most of the time, that is through empty space. But when another media—let's say water or evolution or something I can't even hope to name…even when the name matters so much—gets involved, things change to keep the rule true to the nature of how things really work in the universe. It's not a possibility. It is law.

Maybe what just happened to me was both impossible and inevitable from the perspective of Lagrangian physics. Maybe it minimized the possible actions, making it the only possible next step of action. Why?

Because without a nightlight, despite it being physically impossible in the Grid…the inevitable minimizing action happens. I fall asleep on my own.

Chapter Seven

I DECIDE to keep both all of my future physics lectures and this secret to myself as I wipe the dried-up drool from my arm and stumble behind Faheem—the same giant who just ripped me from the table as if I am his infant and he is a nursemaid monster carrying me safely, if not painfully, through the market.

As law of the universe would have it, the next few minimizing actions take place: I follow Faheem like a wounded sheep, manage to keep my mouth shut, and allow a few critical conclusions to sink into the rapidly evolving synapses in my brain that accommodate to the role I play now—mute miracle boy. Thank G I can't speak as this creep drags me around because if I could, I might have tapped my panic button and screamed, "If I can sleep without spending all my hard-earned V-bucks for the privilege, what else am I working for unnecessarily?"

Another delightful quiver goes through my mind. Only this time, I welcome the black hole instead of getting lost in it. And what I can only guess is probably a fissure in a great wall of glass that surrounds me spreads. I begin to see the illusions of our previous choices fracture around me like I am the broken screen of an iPhone. I remember what my "name" means and laugh—names being so important, as if they predetermine the course of events destined to the *named* before the story even gets started. Guess my name was never any different. Name anagrams out to twenty-three words inside a name. Twenty-three.

"Impossible yet inevitable," I whisper to the director of this movie: *My Story, My Life.*

As we go through the inevitable motions to visit our nap pod, I notice very different things. Why? I finally realize I am not only playing eight chess boards up and down but also side to side simultaneously. I gulp from the pressure of that awareness as I look around for information in ways I have not previously bothered. Every action and non-action I take from this now-moment on, must consider least action principles and how it applies to everything I do in eight times eight directions at once.

Here are a few of the most critical things I ponder or notice. And in order to keep track of them, I engage my thought tracker by tapping my left cheekbone eight times. It's a tool Faheem and I can employ if we disagree about an assignment. I track my observations, and he tracks his. We download the thoughts, delay the decision, and revisit the assignment the following shift after I listen to his thoughts and he listens to mine at a brain, not mouth, level. Quite clever. I imagine the tech implications for future telepathic communications are quite significant. I have to remember to suggest that in my next City Planning Persons report. But then I remember I don't trust where those reports are going anymore, and I will need to delete these thoughts once I get to think about them some more when I am just stuck in my pod doing nothing but not sleeping.

1. All of our groupings are formed via factors of eight…the second "honest number" because it is two cubed. Eight—a Fibonacci number. And the same number visibly upside down or right-side up. Not to mention, turned on its side makes an infinity symbol. Eight—also the same as the number of directional boards in Infinity Chess War—the only video game that Vantage allows us to play. *Interesting*. Not only allows…encourages us to play. *Even more interesting*.

2. All of us wear similar uniforms, the color of our hooded jumpsuit panic buttons establishing our AIP class the only difference. It would be quite hard to notice if a few people in line went missing. In fact, if two of us were taken away, no one would notice except the two in front and the two behind them. *Two times two times two is eight, honestly*.

3. I have only truly spoken at length to Faheem, the two AIPs in front of us, and the girls named Lacie and Celia behind us. Speaking of behind us, Celia's eyes seem dark today. And Lacie keeps whispering to her.

4. No one here ever says or does anything negative. Can I be the only one in the Grid who has negative thoughts? I am also the only person who disconnected from my nap pod. Is that a coincidence? Probably. But I can't seem to recall having negative thoughts or ideas for too many years to count—not since Debbie and her ice cream rescued me after a bad bully day at Trussell Ranch Elem so many years ago.

5. Context really does mean everything. And now that I have a new, upside-down context to view things

from within, the meanings I previously assigned everything have become meaningless. Where I once assumed things were designed in my favor...now, not so much. I should panic because that leads to an awareness that I truly know nothing about nothing. But could that also mean anything previously impossible just became possible because, much like a child determined to explore and challenge all limits, I have no boxed-in thoughts with this indeterminate context? Maybe. *Maybe—with thirty-four words inside it for my thirty-four years.*

6. Lacie is cute. Like really cute. Like no chick in *Best Day Ever* has ever once compared to her cuteness. I wonder why I didn't notice her this much before. Like I forgot to remember how attracted I was to her. Suddenly, I wish it were just she and I and that none of this was real but the two of us and thirty-four maybes...

7. My mind wanders more than it used to. Yet the more my mind wanders, the more clearly I can see where I am standing and what I am doing from a perspective that feels beyond me. It is like...the more my brain drifts while awake, my view goes from a first-person point of view to a more highly evolved view, better described as...mixed. One where both third and first-person overlap and intersect. Did I mention Lacie?

8. Sleep via the nightlight never left me as refreshed as a few hours of spontaneous sleep—which means I have spent years working for the Vantage bucks to earn enough credit to purchase a lesser version of something I already possess within me.

9. The people and process that runs the Grid are

invisible. I look around me for leadership, guards, the officers that answer our panic buttons but cannot see them. Where are they? And why do we plug each other in for dormancy? Who are the last two AIPs in line anyway? Can I safely assume the Grid now runs itself? Are its programs and employees, thanks to Faheem and me, so efficient that they upgrade and maintain and teach themselves? Isn't that what artificial intelligence programs do?

So, I just decide if I am going to learn more about what is really going on in the Grid...while all the others sleep, tonight I must escape.

Chapter Eight

"YOU. FIRST. HAM," I say and try to make it sound like he's the one saying it. "Your. Chick. Awaits." He raises his famous eyebrow but doesn't say much.

"Um-huh. K."

His pupils narrow, so I take it up a level and double the bait. "Wavy skirt. Muscular thighs. Red dress. High heels." He smiles, and I know I have him now because he stares off to the upper right, and his eyes glow with some memory I am thankful not to be privy to.

He nods.

"Sorry. About. Earlier." I plug Faheem in and watch his nightlight illuminate instantly.

I swear I hear him moan, not in an unpleasant way, and chills spread down my back because I do not want to imagine the possibilities of what dormancy is really doing to my BFF while both the synapses in the grey matter of his cortex and the blood in his groin think he's getting laid by what's-her-name.

I climb inside my pod, and Lacie closes the door, grumbling the whole time and never once making eye contact with me. I'd give anything to tell her how much she's in my thoughts, but I can't, so I just wave, which *maybe* she notices…or maybe not. *Lacie, I have way more than thirty-four questions for you. Look at me. Just look at me. See me. Please.*

I wait, twiddling my skinny thumbs, which have condemned so many youths to their occupational fates, for as long as I can stand it. We have an "accident" release button that opens our pod in the rare event of a liquid or solid soiling during one of our reality sleep programs. I press it with my evil thumb of destiny for the first time ever and wait. Moments later, my door opens, revealing a new uniform to replace my old one covered in piss or shit. And I guess it is piss and shit but not the kind that the naked eye can see. My excrement, as invisible to an outsider as the bacteria on my skin that make up my biome.

I quickly fold the new jumpsuit inside my old one and look around rapidly like an erratic factorial in some chaos equation even I can't solve. After a minute or so, I stop shaking my head and wait, taking slow, deep breaths to calm myself down as I make up an excuse for someone to come. No one does. I wait longer. Still no one comes. Eventually, I sit down and look out at all the lights on in all the nap pods in this mega sleep station and marvel at how the elite in our busy Grid are completely asleep while the lower classes toil on with work that never stops, never ends, never rests.

I raise my hood and say my name, hoping to motivate myself to take the next mandatory step. "Jagga." Names being so important, as if they predetermine the course of events destined to the *named* before the story even gets started. "Jagga, remember Jagga means awake. Jagga, wake up." I gag, unable to swallow all the spit forming in my mouth, and vomit out the "j" and "a" and whatever was left of the blue pills I took earlier. Once I take the first step, there will be no turning back.

I stand and start walking, the electric fence ensnaring us behind me as I make my way inward. I pay close attention, carefully recording my path under the dim moonlight—beyond the dormancy pods, along the pathways of nothing but concrete against my soles, weaving through unfamiliar blocks of old abandoned warehouse after warehouse lying in the dark outskirts of the grouping of towering buildings in the center. Each decrepit building seems to tell me a story—a story of their past life; now they appear dead...like the rest of them...when the world as we knew it crumbled. I track my steps, keeping count in my mind as it formulates how long it'll take me to retrace my steps because I will have to get back in time...back before the night's dormancy ends or else my treachery will be discovered. Every step is actually two steps, a step away and the step back. Every minute two minutes. And since I can't afford to get lost, of course, I do. Or not. What does "lost" mean when you have no idea where you are going?

I step over a heap of debris at the edge of the presumably once-bustlingly commercial area, and my foot sinks into the earth. Looking down at the soft, dark soil, I take in the feeling of softness against my soles, the sensation a stark difference from the concrete that covers everywhere else within the Grid. *I haven't seen dirt in...*

As I reach an area that must be the old dried up drainage basin of this region my pant legs are covered in dirt, and I give infinite thanks that I held on to the second precious uniform. Smiling and feeling freer than I can remember, I look up at the face of the moon and compare its location to a few of the more well-known constellations. Alnitak, of Orion's Belt, the brightest O-type star in the entire night's sky, winks, quickly reminding me that I have twenty minutes at most to explore before I must return to basecamp. That's when I realize...

maybe I don't want to go back—back to not living but merely existing within a few square miles of flat earth, nothing but nothing in the distance beyond the electric fences decorating this desolate land of metal-lined captivity.

Chapter Nine

WITH ONLY A FEW moments to spare, I change my uniform, discard the dirty one down a chute to the washing machines, and sit down in this fabulously comfortable chair. Trying to rest briefly with closed eyes but failing, the image of a man, his skin even darker than Faheem's, fills my mind. He says, shaking his fist from his podium, *"The ultimate measure of a man is not where he stands in moments of comfort and convenience but where he stands at times of challenge and controversy. I have a dream..."* Although I don't remember what comes next in his speech, the idea of a dream belonging to a particular individual strikes me as foreign. For years now, the nightlight has formulated my dreams, only the general category mine to choose from. The rest played out for me without my input or explicit consent. "You signed the paper in exchange for the safety of the Grid," I remind myself.

But I have a dream—had a dream, anyway. Can there be a dream of my own that only belongs to me? Can we share a dream? If dreams, creations controlled by the reticular activating system in my brain, don't belong to me, does anything? Wait a minute...nothing belongs to me. The slogan replays. *"If you have something to offer us, we have something to offer you. Vantage, vantage, the only sustainable option that will ever do."*

I vow to leave my dormancy pod again tonight and dig deeper.

Faheem opens my pod and reaches in to pull me out like a piece of toasted wheat bread. *Ding.* He grins at me like yesterday never happened. "Dude, almost Christmas. Not much time to shop. What do you want me to gift you that you don't already have?"

Now one of my eyebrows gets all triangular like his usually does. "Aren't you still mad? And get me nothing. Obviously."

"Mad at what?" He squeezes my hand in this back and forth pattern he calls a "special shake"—his displeasure obvious at my inability to remember the order of the steps.

"You mean who." I try to catch on before the "special shake" is over but can never seem to keep up with his perfect rhythm.

"K. At. Who? Or is it whom? I can never remember that rule." He drops my hand.

"Me." I cough and clear my throat.

"For. Like. What?" he asks and twirls me around by the same arm he almost ripped off yesterday. When I say, "Ouch," he acts genuinely surprised I'm sore on that side.

"Screwing up our counts. Complaining. You know. Negative assaultive language. You pressed your red panic butt—"

"What the duck are you going on about? Assaultive language? You are making weird jokes today. Stick to math jokes. Besides, I've never pressed my button. That's ridiculous. When will you learn to stay in *Best Day Ever*? You obviously had a nightmare in another program." He kicks one leg up in the air, the lower leg next and clicks his heels.

"No…I…" But then I decide to just let him play his verbal

chess pieces and tell me more that I don't already know about what did or didn't happen yesterday in linear time. After all, my context is now backward, and I have no idea what board I'm playing on right now. I bite my lip and just chew on it to keep from saying anything else that might affect circumstances moving in so many directions at once. Eight up is eight. Eight down is eight. Eight sideways is infinity.

He giggles. "Life is pointless you know."

I smile. "Only without geometry," I add and pat him on the back.

Lacie waves at me like we are pals again, and Celia seems well-rested, her dark circles completely gone. They are smiling and laughing and…it's like yesterday never happened.

"Give me a replay of our work yesterday," I say. "Just doing a little experiment in observing your word choice."

"Why?"

"So I can"—I swallow—"play a better game of chess against you later."

"K. Sure. Challenge accepted." By now, we are walking not behind one another but side by side as we enter our building for work, an eight-story structure made of nothing but white concrete walls. As we head into our individual stations, each closed by a thick door from the next, and sit down, he says, "Let's see. You made a math joke as usual, which sucked as usual. I did all the work…as usual."

I catch my breath and hold on to the edge of my seat because I'm not sure if this is a joke or he means it.

"Nah, Gag, my love," he continues, "just ragging you. We kicked butt…as usual…because we are the best City Persons Planning experts ever. And because of how amazing we are, I got three extra minutes with that juicy babe in *Best Day Ever,* who put her perfectly round mouth—"

I stop him right there. He has absolutely no memory of what

happened during our fight yesterday, and I don't need to hear about a computer program's pouty mouth to prove it. Only the good parts of yesterday stick in his mind. And the minutes line up perfectly in a straight line through empty space. One extra. The next day, two extras. The next, three. Let me guess. We finish four minutes early today. But if there was another medium, what would happen?

I throw him an easy riddle. "Why are obtuse angles so angry?"

He catches on immediately. "Because they never get to be right." We both laugh, the smile spreading up our faces and taking over our eyes. But unlike his, mine goes back down and gets stuck like unwanted gum at the sides of my mouth because if I am right…if what I think is going on here, angry won't even cut it.

Chapter Ten

THE FOLLOWING DAY GOES WELL, all things considered. We make our designations, listing out the best occupations and expected life plans for so many youths before us. Our thumbs of doom sign the contracts and "make it so" with five minutes to spare and one day before Christmas to motivate us to come back tomorrow. We take our supplements and follow our diets perfectly tailored to sustain our bodies to the greatest extent possible for the longest number of years. We travel through doors and places and do nothing at all as another day goes by. For fun, we "play" Infinity Chess War, marching through yet another example of what happens on boards in eight directions upwards and sideways when players move their pieces, always doing nothing at all as another day goes by.

Faheem drops first into a false reality that he is both addicted to and robbed by while I drop out entirely—false rewards so meaningless outside the context of the place that serves them to its willing victims. Much like owning tickets to the rides at a circus that has left my town and gone on to the next, I look at the V-bucks in my account and feel sick at how much the useless currency has cost me.

"Buyer's remorse...inevitable," I say to Faheem's nightlight as it glows on, and he hums in ecstasy completely unaware of how expensive his *drug of choice* really is. Mine are no different in essence once the particulars are stripped away—anagrams, math, a complex game of chess no more valuable than an action- and sex-packed adventure in *Best Day Ever* except to the one who treasures it so.

Celia's eyes behind us grow dark again, and Lacie ignores me once more, forever trapped in the illusion of trying to save someone unwilling to participate in their own rescue. The perfectly un-winnable battle for a healer who never stops giving too much. The infinite motivator for someone who might classify as a Supporter, subclass SW—Social Worker like Lacie. An AIP who has given too much of themselves as their drug of choice

"AIP, Artificially Integrated Person," I whisper. "AIP, come get your banana while I swing out of this tree."

My pod opens, and I take the extra suit and escape to go find the place I once called home. I imagine it looks exactly the same as I now so clearly remember it amongst the crumbling walls and disintegrating IKEA furniture.

I travel to the farthest northwest corner of the Grid—where any other traveler would never know an old, upscale residential community existed if they didn't know how to disable the projection screen that makes this corner look just like the rest of the Grid. But I do. I remember the screen, the device, the reset button—all of it.

Expecting why already on some Lagrangian-elegant level but still trying to hide it from myself at the level of linear time, why...why anyone would hide this region of the Grid, I enter my old home. Modern by the standards of the year 2030, it is lovely, and the familiar joy of being somewhere I love so much soothes me in a way no calculus equation or prime number could. Everything untouched from the clear images in my mind of this four-thousand-plus square foot mansion except one. Only one tiny thing, something so easily unnoticed by anyone other than me, has gone missing.

Tomorrow, I will say goodbye to Faheem and Lacie and leave for good. If I tell them, they won't remember, so one last day with them...it's just for me—my own little Christmas gift to myself. Selfish, maybe. But now, that's all I've got left.

Chapter Eleven

MY FINAL MORNING in the Grid, a happy and hopeful Faheem yanks me from my nap pod. I am tired, of course, but refuse to let it get to me. Extra Shatterproof and Ginseng keep me operating at an acceptable level to convince Faheem we really did finish our evaluations six minutes early. We assign somewhere between fifty and sixty youth to occupational positions today with a short lunch break to play a round of Infinity Chess War that now humors more than motivates me.

Mid-session with one of the girls, an obvious artistic genius to us, I say to my occupational partner, "How do we know she's real?"

"Real?" He snorts. "What crazy theory are you testing out on me now?"

"No, I mean it. We keep assuming she comes first and our evaluation of her comes second. But what if the order of events were reversed to minimize some action we haven't as yet considered, like swimming through muddy water?" I frown. "Or some devious plot we haven't uncovered, yet still are minimizing without our knowledge of it."

"What are you on about? Do not try to explain Langrangian

mechanics to me with this question…please. For G's sake, you suck at explaining complex physics theory. It is your greatest weakness."

Grinning, I give him a high-five across the desk because he's correct from several overlapping contexts, and that is funny to a guy who loves bad math jokes and plans on escaping the Grid for good tonight.

I stand up, roll my neck, and suck on my bottom lip for a minute. "The aliens understood physics just fine, but whatever, my friend."

He shakes his head and thinks I'm kidding, but I'm not. I remember the movie, the book, all those songs the nightlight has stolen from him. *Mary, did you know?*

He presses a button, and our desk rises to match his height instead of mine. I climb onto a stool, and now we are both level in this momentary reality—even though I realize we can never be level when his memories are stolen and mine still remain. Level—such a relative term from the perspective of my new role as director of *My Story, My Life* while Faheem just plays along as he always has, completely unaware that he already knows how this ending ends.

The fifteen monitors, continually giving us various forms of data to integrate about the candidate before us, shift position to accommodate the most possible comfort for our necks should we look in any direction from our similar but completely different level.

I explain myself. "Seriously. What if our evaluation comes first, and then she comes second?"

"Not. Getting. Your. Meaning. That's. Absurd." He throws back a shot of wheatgrass and hands me one.

"Are there any extra protein bars over there?"

"Sure," he says. "But you hate them."

"Everything is relative, even hate." *So true*. I sigh. "I bet you a million V-bucks that tomorrow I love them."

He hands me eight, and I take them and keep going with what will be my final occupational assessment. The monitors speed up with information about her DNA, her biome, her family of origin, and they keep asking us to answer questions that get more specific each time than the last. The program makes us tell it in what she will excel, in what she will fail, how long she will live—the list of particulars seemingly endless for this girl. Sometimes with a particular candidate, I get a few screens. Sometimes they go on and on—like that boy with the odd birthmark we sent to biohazard washing.

I turn to Faheem. "What if she isn't real and we are teaching them how to make her? What if they are showing us a digital version of a desired product/object/AIP and we are explaining to them why and how and which ingredients to use to make her?"

"You have become chaos theory," he replies and pinches my arm.

"Exactly," I say. "My point, exactly. Wouldn't you want her if you were the Grid?"

"They already have her. I mean, we. We have her. See— she's right there."

"Is she? Can you be sure? For. Reals. Can you?"

He sighs and rolls his eyes. "What happened to you, my brother?"

I whisper so softly that he hardly hears me. "You broke my nightlight. That's what happened. You punched me in the back. It broke. Now I can't access the sleep programs. The nightlight is Vantage proprietary technology, and I am starting to think it is—"

A loud sound down the hall makes me jump. My heart skips a beat, certain I am discovered. But the sound passes, and no one comes to take me away. Quickly I add, "Now I remember everything. Now I question everything."

He swallows. "Absurd. I would remember hurting you, Gag."

"They brainwashed you into forgetting." We put our thumbs together to make our assessment official—piano virtuoso, touring classical jazz musician.

The door opens, and Lacie comes running in, tears streaming down her face.

"Celia?" I ask, after remembering the dark circles under her partner's eyes and how a drama like this would affect the autonomic nervous system of someone addicted to helping someone in distress. Faheem holds on to my thumb but won't let go, as though we only have one thumb between us.

Lacie wipes her face and locks eyes with me. "She's disappeared. And I've received an urgent memo to report to the eighth floor by eight a.m. or my V-bucks will also disappear for good. They've wiped my account. Told me to go a night without sleep. That it would help me make my decision tomorrow." She collapses at my feet and sobs. "Without money, I'll never sleep again. I want to keep her secrets. But how do I choose between her and sleep? Help me. Do you have any extra money? I am so tired." She trembles but more like a drug addict than an injured person whose loyalty is obviously being tested by a corporation that imprisons her in a web designed just for her.

"What did he look like? The one who took her away?" I ask.

"Hmmm. His face was blank. I'm not sure he was an AIP. Maybe he was a robot or something."

"Did he have a gun?"

She squints her eyes. "A what?"

"Never mind. How old?"

She looks side to side and then down. "Hard to say. Maybe sixteen."

Maybe. These are not the thirty-four maybes I want to have with her.

"Describe anything about him you can. Anything. Anything, for G's sake." I shake her hard, hoping it will jolt her memory.

"I don't know. No, wait. There was one thing. A mark on his arm. It was red." She pauses.

"Like a letter?" I ask, hoping she will say no but already knowing that she won't.

"How did you...? Like an F. Yes."

"I didn't. But now I do." I take a deep breath. The plan just changed because the media reflecting things just got more serious.

"Help me, Jagga," she begs. "Please."

"I can help but not in the way you think," I add...because subtracting will never do. "Faheem, grab a bottle of lavender oil, some chamomile chew tabs, and a few sprigs of mint."

Lacie grabs her stomach and stands up, still partially bent over. "Anything you can do to help."

I rub the lavender on her back, and the touch of her skin is so familiar I swear I know the feel of it—so soft and silky— even better than my own. "Impossible," I whisper. "How can I remember the curve of your back?" I hold on to my breath because now I'm drowning in so much muddy water that empty space has become impossible.

She gasps, and a zing of intensity travels back and forth between us like we just invented the first video game, Pong. "You can't."

"I have to. G...Grid...help me."

"No, you are helping me."

"Am I?" I ask completely confused by what is happening.

She smiles. Even turned around, I feel her lips widen and her cheeks go up despite the pain I suspect she feels in her heart.

"But that's the spot you used to touch me, when... What? Sorry. That's ridiculous. I am just so upset."

But it is possible. And it is her favorite spot. I am as sure of my memory now as the *pi* out to thirty-four digits, and all thirty-four *maybes* return to me because she just ate a slice of me. I am also sure of the next minimizing action because our muddy water rippled through eight boards up and eight boards across like a tsunami.

"There's a flat mole just over your right…"

She silently stands up straight and takes a deep breath before pushing all the air back out. "My breast."

"You're the one who took it—the picture from the house. You took it." I breathe in trying to capture as much of the air she just let out as possible like it is the last breath I will ever need. Even though I know that is ridiculous. I will never catch her air and am already taking another breath while I am thinking about how the last one was probably my very last one. Let's face it…some force greater than me drives the air in and out of me. In and out. In and out. Over and over. It breathes me, so how could I breathe her?

"Took what?"

But I see it through the back of her head, feel the tension in her body because of it—the lie. Her illusion shatters so slightly she would call it uncertainty more than a lie. But it's a lie, no doubt. Her physical body knows even though the lies in her head are trying to steal the truth from her. A lie Vantage forced upon her through slogans and subliminal messages and programming that I must undo.

The greater force that breathes me blows the air out of my lungs once more. "A photo of a bouquet of white—"

"Roses. It's on my desk. I don't know how I got it." The lie sprouts roots and digs in.

"I do."

"Turn around," I tell her. "Trust me. I won't fail you again." And that is no lie.

"My legs are shaking, and I feel like the need to sleep is taking over," she says, but all I can manage to focus on is how I remember her legs on me, something else entirely taking over.

"I still love you. Turn around. Swallow the chamomile. Roll the mint sprig between your teeth and bite down," I tell my wife. How could we have forgotten we were once married and that her wedding bouquet was made of white roses?

She does as I say. "Somehow," she mumbles, the mint making it hard for her to pronounce things clearly, "I trust you. I knew you were the one to turn to. I've always known I can trust you. Like you are mine and I am yours...but that's crazy."

"No, it's not. Bite down. Things are about to get uncrazy."

Faheem has been standing there speechless. I wave him toward me. He comes, unable to deny my requests at a time like this.

"Don't say a word, Ham. Just hit her under her right shoulder blade as hard as you can. Trust me, buddy. Hit her now. Her life depends on it. And now, so does yours."

Before she turns around, he does exactly as I ask, and I can only hope the eight cycles of pain she suffers are less terrible than mine were. As she drops to the floor, I lock eyes with the best friend I have ever had...both before I signed my Vantage agreement and after they used it against me, and say to him, "Now find a large pipe or rod or something that I can hit you with next."

Chapter Twelve

THERE ARE NOW three of us awake in a sleeping world. We are fugitives undiscovered, but together we are greater than one plus one plus one. Perhaps we are three factorial, 3!

At least that's what I think until I see Faheem fall apart like a properly cooked pot roast on the end of a fork poisoned by reality program withdrawal. Slobbering like an infant getting new teeth, he keeps pounding the side of his nap pod, demanding I let him out. I go to him, hoping, pleading with Grid that no one hears him. *Mary, don't you hear?*

"Quiet. Please, Ham, be quiet." I give him my sweetest eyes.

"I. Can't. Make. It. Help." The drool drips down the side of his mouth, and he wipes most of it away. One sticky, white strand refuses to leave him and makes its presence known every time he tries to unlock his jaw, probably stuck from grinding his teeth so hard.

"Man. You have it bad. Way worse than I did. How many programs do you run each night? Two? Maybe three?" I scratch my head trying to figure out what will calm his nerves enough for us to take off. From my calculations, we have another hour left at most. Then we have to go, and I can't leave him like this. He will never make it.

"Two? Are you fucking kidding me?" He coughs, and the smell of urine fills the pod.

"How many?" I ask, getting exponentially more worried by the second. I need to check on Lacie and see if she has stopped crying about Celia yet. "How many, Ham? Honestly."

"I loop my bitch all night. At least ten times. At least."

"Holy! Shit! Ten!" Finally, I understand why he uses the broken sentences like that.

He punches his own face to unlock his jaw, and the smell of feces floods the tiny space. "Dude. Sorry. I'm. Dying. For. Reals."

I hand him a new grey uniform and adjust the controls on his essential oils while I think about all the times he got so nervous right before drop. His florid addiction is so obvious in retrospect…like the time he smacked me in the back that started this whole series of minimizing events in nonlinear motion. The irony is not lost on me as much as the time is, so I forgo my usual laugh and decide Lacie needs me more than this junkie.

When I get to her, she is just lying back, eyes closed and sighing. "How long have we been here? Do you remember yet?"

Mary, do you know?

I shake my head. "No idea."

"K. Can he travel?"

I shake my head again.

"Then we plug him back in, or we lose him for good. As usual, he's your greatest weakness."

Now it's my turn to pull her out like a pickle from a jar.

She mutters under her breath. "Never me. Always him. One time, I wish it were me."

Together, we approach Faheem's pod and assess the

damage. It's fair to say he's not okay and is not going to be. How will I carry him? My eyes dart around like protons and neutrons seeking a way out of our predicament that doesn't exist. A wheelchair. A scooter. Anything that will make him mobile. To save Lacie, we will have to leave him and come back for him later, or we have to stay and let her face leadership in a few short hours.

"Turn on your right side slowly," Lacie says and adjusts Faheem's neck. He sighs deeply, and all the muscles in his body relax. His spittle increases, and I reach over and wipe it for him.

Throwing away his soiled clothes, I ask my bride, "What did you do to him exactly?" still trying to find a way to carry him even if he weighs almost twice as much as I do.

"You learn a few tricks taking care of the misfits. Social Worker is a tough occupation. Surely an elite Persons Planner like you understands what I do for a living…always making sacrifices for people who can never repay me. It's my nature, remember?" She smiles, and for a second I think the sun might pop out of her face and blind me. "I mean what I did for a living. This match is over, the last few plays obvious to me now."

"That's Infinity Chess talk, my love," I say, trying to find a way to apologize for what's happening because I guess this isn't the first time Faheem has come between us.

"Of course it is. Or eight on its side talk. Either way you look at it, you get the same result." She puts her hand on my shoulder. "Hey, you, I remember one of your favorite jokes. Why can't atheists solve exponential equations?"

I puff out my nostrils slightly and let a crooked smile knock my face off its x-axis. "Because they don't believe in higher powers."

"Exactly. God knows that."

"God. Not Grid. G means God, not Grid," I whisper and allow God to breathe me. *Mary, I don't know what to do next.*

Feeling like the ultimate failure, I close Faheem's door and vow to find a way to make this up to him, my Infinity Chess War partner, and to her, too. I turn to Lacie, and we kiss for the first time in...well...a while. The embrace feels so good we lose track of what time we have left to escape. The sun peeks over her head, and the day breaks on Christmas morning.

Chapter Thirteen

WHILE SHE FACES eight shadows on eight life-sized monitors accusing her of treachery, I face child after child after child who I shall condemn to a life addicted to this poison or that one, and my thumbs ache in a way words cannot do justice to describe.

Faheem is tired, moving more slowly than usual but has no memory of what happened last night. It breaks my heart what I cannot tell him. It breaks my heart it is our last day together, our last chess game, our last everything. Unless... "Unless"—such an uncertain word in every possible context or direction at a time like this.

A few hours later, I march with my best friend for the last time, certain in every possible context and direction that if my plan has been discovered, everyone in my mega sleep station will pay dearly, especially him. As I march, I think back on how much has changed in such a short period of time.

In a final moment of self-pity, I go back to when...I used to think the worst thing that could happen to a person was being denied dormancy or being exiled off the Grid. But I was such a fool. Turns out, that old saying about perspective being everything...was right. Something unspeakable, something far worse than exile has already happened to me. Too many nights to count, actually. And to think, I signed up for it. So did all the others by the way. It's funny how the very thing you think is helping you can be what hurts you most—before you get a clue, before you decode the whole program *they* are running or can recover from an addiction you didn't even know you had.

So many lies hidden in plain sight make them hard to see. Not many people know that. One lie is easy to notice. But thousands, millions…not so much.

Unable to resist the pull of wanting to help so many others who, unlike me, don't know where we are really going…I look at the lines of us and shiver. Lines and lines of thousands of AIPs, Artificially Integrated Persons—lines and lines of white lies formed in perfect patterns, perfect illusions in perfect sight.

The chicken skin on my arms reminds me to look straight ahead, to help Lacie, Faheem, and myself first, to not avert my gaze, to walk confidently forward toward my final dormancy or else. Or else what I can't say. The watershed? The zones beyond that? Death? Torture? Can any life I imagine be any more torture-filled than this?

Yet no one notices, no one stops us, and no one even seems to care. All the AIPs go to get their meaningless reward that means so much to them. Since leadership is nowhere to be found, Lacie and I do the only thing I can think of. We go home.

Chapter Fourteen

OUR HOME IS VIRTUALLY untouched by anything more menacing than a few wild animals and Father Time. Things are where we left them: fashionably designed chairs from the 2030s at the easy-to-assemble recycled-materials table from IKEA, unused organic towels in the dusty and rusted eco-friendly machine that never finished washing them, Tesla solar shingles still attached to the roof despite the years that have forgotten their value. Everything is how it should be other than the picture that must have been taken the last time we were here. *Last time we were here—the last time we fought our way back to each other...fought the prison we created to save us all.* The thought still hovers as she kisses me but quickly passes because my Persian cucumber gets the better of me.

My bride and I lie down on our old mattress and do what people do at moments like that in a place like this—we remind our bodies how much they have missed each other, and we fall spontaneously and completely asleep until the following morning. Before she awakens, the LED lights outside just barely creeping through the window, I throw on my old favorite hoodie and tiptoe into the kitchen, hoping not to wake her. The soft gray material of this jacket, as comfortable as it always has been, embraces me in familiarity and the unconditional love of a treasured pet, the cuffs unraveling and permanently stained by overuse—too much for any machine to be able to clean it properly. I chuckle softly wondering how many times I've worn it, how many times my hands have waited in the center threadbare pocket as some black, lovely liquid brews. If only I could find some—real coffee, pure black gold. I rustle through the kitchen drawers, looking for an old bag of dark French roast—our favorite. Luckily, I find it, the next medium that I shall allow to alter the course of events by minimizing them—the aroma of old, freeze-dried, but real, coffee. As it brews, I place my hands on the dark brown wood table, running them along the smooth surface and across the scrolled edges on the tops of the decorative legs, taking in all the scents—smoky, bittersweet, hints of caramel—the finest the USDA Organic had before…before we did what we did.

As the carafe fills and the precious grounds soak, a million memories assault me of our lives before, and I sit down in my chair to take them all in. I remember. I remember it all—who I am, who she is…how this came to be.

My hands tremble slightly atop this piece of furniture that could be ten or two hundred years old—steady, well made, and handsome by any era's standards. To stop my growing tremor, I put my hands in the pockets. My fingers, knowing this fold of cloth as well as they know my wife's body, go right to the center—to the place I always kept my most prized possession while we read our novels or watched our movies together. She preferred documentaries or mysteries. Me—science fiction. I pop up my hood and twirl this tiny thing round and round in my hand like I suffer a bridegroom's best version of Tourette's syndrome. This platinum circle has been waiting so long for me —a symbol of my greatest achievement, convincing her to marry me—inside the warm fold of my best old pal, this hooded sweatshirt.

I feel her behind me before I hear her. How long she's been watching I couldn't hope to know. "Shit. You found the real coffee, didn't you?" she asks, and I open my eyes to see her frown like I didn't load the dishwasher as well as she would have.

"And this." I hold out the ring, and she quickly steals it away from me. "Hey," I say, complaining with my lips pursed, hoping she will feel sorry for me and give it back. No such luck. I follow her over to my old desk, then around the table and back again. Our game of cat and mouse goes on for a bit, both of us knowing she always wins.

She pins me against my desk, leaning her body into me. "It's mine now." She laughs, drawing out the end until it ends up more like a sigh. "I was hoping only I would remember it all this time and you would just understand part of what we did to ourselves." She twirls the ring between her fingers and slips it on. "Even if it's no less terrible, you might feel it less terribly."

"You...always trying to keep people from hurting. I love you."

She reaches for me, sliding my hood off with a sweep of her graceful hand as her fingers thread through my not-enough hair. "Ditto."

"Squared." I kiss her smile and wrap her in my arms as she leans in deeper before reluctantly pulling away. My eyes stay closed a moment longer, trying to engrave the feel of her touch into my memory, knowing it won't keep.

I push off from the desk and turn to face it, another medium taking hold—the center drawer. I sit in my office chair and lean back, the old metal base creaking in complaint with me because I do not want to open it. "How long do we have?" I steady myself and pull the handle to face my enemy, a small, white envelope—the final proof that will confirm what I already know is true...because after all, my little bit of Lagrangian candy was so delicious and true to its nature. *Some part of me always knew how this story would end. Mary, I am sure.*

"Minutes to hours. Maybe. I expect the former. But does it matter? Linear time is meaningless. You know that." She sits on my lap and holds me tightly for a few moments before standing back up and walking around the dining room, looking at old pictures and books. She bites her lip a few times as she circles the room twice. I see her play with my ring some more, shaking her head in that slight way she does that always tells me yes or no before her lips do.

"Maybe." I close my eyes and toss the letters around in my mind before I really have to look at what *maybes*, which were obviously convincingly purported to the Vantage board, must have sounded like. Maybe apocalypse, maybe unsurvivable global warming after the rainforests burned down, mercury-poisoned fish and water supply, crops devoid of nutrition, rampant infertility... Did those in power give the good people of Earth enough chances? Could humans have solved our global problems some other way? Was the Grid the only possible cure? Maybe. Maybe not. Now we never will ever know on the other side of just enough convincing *maybes* to allow Vantage Corp. to do so many terrible things to so many innocent people under the guise of saving them. "There are thirty-four words in 'maybe,'" I say as if she doesn't already know that.

I feel my gorgeous woman pause, probably in front of some old collectible item, and mourn the loss of what could have been instead of what already has been. She lingers in front of one shelf longer than the others and sticks something quickly in her pocket. I don't see what it is but realize this is exactly how she got the photo. What a smart and delightful creature she is.

"I've used that maybe line before, haven't I?" I'm still smiling, but at her cleverness, not mine.

"Maybe." She laughs, and I am certain I married the right woman even if I only get to have her for a few hours here and there out of so many possible, but lost, years. "At least thirty-four times."

"There are eighty-six words inside of 'Vantage,'" I say and turn the envelope over to read the address label, hoping that it says something different this time. But nope. It never does. As I wonder how many times I've done this, I feel the sweetness of imaginary candy in my mouth. I already knew—impossible, yet inevitable every single time it happens.

"Yep. That makes nine plus eighty-six for you and twenty-four plus eighty-six for me." She sits down and buries her head in her lap. "Can't be much more than thirty or forty minutes left together now, I expect. Hand me that envelope opener when you are done with it please."

"Okay. It's a lousy weapon, but okay. Now I wish we had been in support of mega guns. We could use like eight right now." I smile at the idea of me holding up an AR-15 and pointing it at the AIPS coming to get us, trying to find some light in the darkness that just consumed us both.

"You and your…'I'll never have a gun' BS really sucks right now. Not fair."

"Well, I still don't think it's fair that 'Jagga' and 'Lacie' could have such different counts of words inside them even though they have the same number of letters." I roll the letter of her name around for a sweet tender moment because I still hate big guns, even if one could save me right now. L-A-C-I-E. Twenty-four words inside her name. Names being so important, as if they predetermine the course of events destined to the *named* before the story even gets started. Funny how other names can be inside of names, I have to admit. And then it dawns on me not who but what her partner really is. "Celia?" I whisper, once more remembering the dark circles under *Lacie's* recently disappeared partner's eyes and how a drama like that would affect the autonomic nervous system of someone addicted to helping others in distress.

She smiles, and it travels up to her eyes and bounces off every star that ever shined. "Both the NRA and numbers can be deceiving. But a name is a name—forward, backward, or even all mixed up," she replies and rushes over to yank the letter and opener from my hand...because she figured out not who but what her occupational partner was while I was still snoring. But I have already looked at the piece of expensive white paper. It's too late. The words are there as plain as day:

Drs. Celia and Jagga Vantage, acting CEOs of Vantage Corp.

I read the letter and the attached unanimously approved version of the contract she and I must have written for our heroic, if not terribly misguided, purposes all those years ago. It's boring, if truth be told, what words the Board of Directors used to approve our project. My project. Celia's project. Our project. Such simple language to describe the Grid she and I designed to save our world on the edge of the apocalypse, the same program from which we cannot seem to escape now even though the dangers that made us create it are long gone at this point. Guess the effects of our perfect planning, a media that even I couldn't possibly predict all the implications of in eight directions up and eight directions over, form the ultimate least action principle—a loop that even its makers cannot find a way to escape.

"How many soldiers do you think we sent to reintegrate us when we found our way out?"

She sighs. "I'm thinking...eight." She slips the letter opener in her back pocket.

But I know the goons that are coming to rescue us from escaping the Grid at our own previous order will have mega big guns. Maybe swords. Maybe both. "I would have thought eight guards in a safety loop to catch myself would be funny, ironic under the circumstances. And that letter opener isn't going to keep one of them off of us. But I love you for trying to save us like you once tried to beat me in chess. Worst thing you could do with that sharp and pointy weapon of mass destruction is stab me."

"But sometimes what seems like a move on one board is actually a move on another board. And not all weapons of mass destruction are as obvious as one might think. Forest, not trees, matters as far as I am concerned," she says and grins. Then she takes my hand and begins to sing a song—one we both know so well, one that will play on an eternal loop in the back of my mind as an a cappella version, my favorite version, until it wakes me up again. Until I remember my name and hers. Jagga means awake. Celia means heavenly. So perfect, whole, and complete. Names being so important, as if they predetermine the course of events destined to the *named* before the story even gets started. Guess the game's name is no different. *Mary, please forgive me. I knew not what I was doing.*

They kick in the door, and all eight of them surround us. But we do not look at them. We do not bother to make sure they all look like identical AIPS, more robot than human, based on the designs of the very program I wrote for the purpose of creating the right AIP for the right job in the Grid. We don't even glance at these AIPS I myself have invented, who will all have the beginnings of a beard shadow, bulging genitalia, a high forehead, muscular arms that hang lower than I would expect at first, and a unique birthmark on one arm that I used to stamp them. Blood red, it almost looks like the letter "T." Or maybe an "F" for fighter.

No, we don't waste another moment being sure. Instead, we choose a few more moments of maybe. Maybe we can dance for all infinity. Maybe they will let us go this time. Maybe I put some escape code in our program to let us out. Maybe. Maybe. And Celia, my forever bride, sings to me as though her song will maybe never end. And we embrace one last eternal second while they inject first me and then her with something that will bring us back into the Grid for another round of Infinity Chess. And just before I lose consciousness, I feel something sharp and pointy stab me in the fat around my belly button. Then I feel my beloved shove something small and firm and round under the skin she just opened up with her blade. Something like a ring, maybe.

Maybe next time we play our own game, we will win.

Maybe...

The End.

About the Author

A. Nicky Hjort is originally from the greater Dallas-Fort Worth area of Texas. She writes stories that cross multiple genre lines, from paranormal romance to Sci-Fi thrillers and back again. And in some subtle way, all of her manuscripts are connected, with their purpose to explore all facets of love and what it has to teach us. Her journey into writing began with her clinical background as a medical doctor when she wrote her first fictional short story about medicine. She hasn't stopped writing since.

Facebook author page:
https://www.facebook.com/Author.A.N.Hjort
Twitter: @A_NickyHjort
Website: **www.anickyhjortbooks.com**
Blog: **www.ANickyHjortBooks.com**
Instagram: **https://www.instagram.com/nickyhjort**

Also by A NICKY HJORT

A Sinister Bouquet: Awakening Book 1: Devyn Mitchell has a choice… listen to the voice of her unborn baby – or die- again. After a near death experience, Doctor Devyn Mitchell finds herself not only mysteriously pregnant but able to communicate with her fetus. She has two choices: give in to total madness or surrender to her new reality, which just may be the only way she and her family will survive the obsessions of the Homeless Hunter's mind. A true paranormal romantic thriller, A Sinister Bouquet: Awakening, the first of the Sinister Series, will take you right to the edge of what you know to be possible and then drop you in a place so dark, so terrifying, that the only passageway out is through the blinding light of awakening. Wake up. Open your eyes. Finally. We've missed you so. (MA18+ for graphic sexual and violent content)

A Sinister Vision: Know This Much is True – Book 2: Elise Phillips, a doctor in training, has successfully repressed her kidnapping five years prior. The only problem is...she has six and one half days to remember every terrible detail, or a total stranger will die. But to make matters even worse, in order to save this nameless woman, Elise will have to face something that scares her even more than death–intimacy. Another paranormal romantic thriller, A Sinister Vision: Know This Much is True, the second of the Sinister Series, will take you even further over the edge of what you know to be possible and guide you right back out through the only way left...impossible. Wake up. Open your eyes. Accept your assignment.... The problem is not to find the answer–but to face it. Know this much is true.

(MA18+ for graphic sexual and violent content)

Where Tyndra Turns to Ardnyt – The Norn Novellas: In the center of a magical world there grows a beautiful and terrible chasm of climbing plants. On one side of the Ivy Wall we find the hell-of-Tyndra, on the other, the heaven-of-Ardnyt. But legend has it that in the middle…lives a preternatural beast that imprisons and tortures the children from both sides. When the war against time begins, Azza will have to cross over the Ivy Wall, something that has never been done before by a living being. But if she does make it through, she just might discover who she really is and how she became trapped in this alternate reality. A fairytale at heart, this is the first chapter in the epic saga of the youngest and most fickle of the four Norn Sisters. The same feisty immortal creature who must escape her inherent inner darkness to learn the meaning of love. A veritable palindrome from start to finish, the narrative of Where Tyndra Turns to Ardnyt journeys through duality to discover what shocking truths emerge when up becomes down, life becomes death, suffering becomes release, and the most unexpected endings become the most surprising beginnings. Welcome to a place where forwards and backwards are exactly the same direction. Here Where Tyndra Turns to Ardnyt.

The City: The Jane Harvest: Winning battles means Ink honors, prestige, and life itself. …Yet nobody understands what losing truly means. On another planet two hundred years in the future, twenty-one-year-old Isla Jane struggles helplessly to figure out who she is and what her world really means. Marked with a forbidden tattoo of the rising sun, she is a natural champion of humanity and a gifted warrior in Heats– lavish battles fought in the conjoined minds of the participants for the morbid amusement of the masses. Despite Isla's desire to fade into the background, she emerges as an obvious leader of her people when the senseless assassination of a youth forces her to face the truth.Her volatile world, disguised by its elaborate battles and constant mayhem, is a prison without bars and a coffin, the lid already half-closed, that they must escape. But when she vows to find a way to bring her people back home, Isla will have to deconstruct consciousness and the very nature of the space time continuum to unravel good from evil, truth from lies, and survival from true love. Welcome to the City–where it takes lives to save lives…

Also from the Lavish Publishing family

Irrevocable Series
Samantha Jacobey
http://myBook.to/TheIrrevocableSeries

The end of the world is coming, or so they say, and that puts
Bailey Dewitt on a crash course with Armageddon. Orphaned,
she and her young brothers find themselves living with their
renegade uncle as part of a group of survivalists. She struggles
against them, searching for a way to escape, but every
discovery only terrifies her more.

For Caleb Cross, the Ranch is a way of life. The members of
their group are family, and none should come between them.
Smitten from the moment he met Bailey, his choices are no
longer easy, his path no longer clear. He wants to welcome her
and the twins into their fold and hopes his kin will agree.

But the elders who lead them aren't interested in the trouble-
some girl. They are plotting for the time they will be rid of her

and expect Caleb to go along with their plans - he is after all one of them.

At first, Bailey resists Caleb's charms, but soon must admit that she desperately needs a friend. She has no intention of anything more, but when the elders make their move, she is forced to trust him with her very life.

They both have hard lessons to learn. Relationships built on secrets and lies don't come with guarantees. When the world falls apart around them, some things are Irrevocable.

Rosinanti Series
Kevin J. Kessler
http://myBook.to/RosinantiSeries

The Rosinanti Dragons are no more. Since their extinction nearly one thousand years ago these primal powerhouses have fallen into the obscurity of history's forgotten lore. In that time, humans have come to dominate the world of Terra, peacefully ignorant to one horrifying truth: ancient evil stirs around them, waiting to reclaim its lost world.

For Valentean Burai, animus warrior of the kingdom of Kack-ritta, the details surrounding humanity's victory over the Rosinanti are more than just a history lesson. The long-buried mysteries of this archaic conflict may hold the answers that he has so desperately sought regarding his own past.

As the awful truth of the Rosinanti's supposed demise comes to light, Valentean must stand together with Seraphina, a magically gifted princess, to embark upon a mission to maintain order and light throughout Terra. Only together can these two lifelong friends face down the resurgence of the Rosinanti legacy and combat the greatest threat their world has ever known.